We marched along the [...]
trees. Diane was to n[...]
involved in our practice[...]
to the sea on my right, [...]
of emulating Rod Melville during my two visits to
the hole in the Skins Game. My attention was
diverted from my caddie and I forgot all about
her until I heard her cry of alarm. By the time I
turned to her, it was far too late.

She was being bundled into the trees by two
figures in denims, T-shirts and black balaclavas.
Before I could even try to help her, something
soft and pungent was clamped over my mouth by
an unseen assailant. His other arm was around
my neck and I fought to shake him off my back
but my resistance wilted. Red-hot needles shot up
my nostrils and down my throat. My lungs were
on fire, my mind was a furnace and my limbs
refused to function.

I was being burned alive.

Golf was over for the day.

KEITH MILES

Green Murder

SPHERE BOOKS LIMITED

A *Sphere* Book

First published in Great Britain in 1990 by
Macdonald & Co (Publishers) Ltd
London & Sydney
Published by Sphere Books Ltd 1991

Printed and bound in Great Britain by
BPCC Hazell Books
Aylesbury, Bucks, England
Member of BPCC Ltd.

ISBN 0 7221 6118 2

Sphere Books Ltd
A Division of
Macdonald & Co (Publishers) Ltd
165 Great Dover Street,
London SE1 4YA

A member of Maxwell Macmillan Publishing Corporation

To my son, Conrad,
a wonderful caddie to have by your side
both on and off a golf course

Learn the fundamentals of Golf
SWINGING SWEARING CHEATING
Practice balls 5/– a bucket
Some of them round

Sign at Manly Golf Club, Sydney
1911

CHAPTER ONE

I SUPPOSE IT HAD TO happen sooner or later but it still hurt me deeply. That was her intention. She rang at the worst possible moment. I was sitting at my little table in Carnoustie, wrestling with my VAT return, trying to reduce three whole months of anarchic life to neat columns of figures. Mathematically, I'm not a convincing liar. It was a gruesome chore and not helped by the fact that I had, as usual, left it until the eleventh hour. We were parked in a gateway down a quiet country lane in Berkshire. Nobody was about. Even the birds were muted. Facing up to the reality of my financial situation is something that I can only do in the utmost privacy.

I was soon invaded. The telephone interrupted me and threw my calculations into disarray. I snatched up the receiver in a foul mood.

'Alan?'

It was Rosemary. Her voice was a cocktail of charm, hostility and polite malice. With plenty of ice.

'What do you want?' I grunted.

'I have something important to tell you.'

'That makes a change.'

'Don't be sarcastic.'

'Then don't provoke my sarcasm.'

Her famous sigh. 'Must you be so tedious, Alan?'

'Get to the punchline.'

'It's very tiresome.'

'State your business and depart gracefully.'

'I'm going to get married.'

The words were like a mallet on my eardrum. My head echoed with pain and I was overcome with such a sense of betrayal that my eyes filled with tears. It was ludicrous. Rosemary had every right to get married again. We'd been divorced for years now and there was no legal barrier to hold her back. By the same token, I had a good reason to want her to find another husband. It would be wonderful to have someone to take the emotional strain off me, not to mention the monetary burdens. In theory, the news should have come as a blessed relief.

And yet I was wounded. I was angry, lonely, suddenly desperate. Could I be – no, it was unthinkable – jealous? As I slumped over the table in my motor caravan, I felt like an old stuffed sack that has just been expertly ripped apart during bayonet practice.

'Alan?' She jabbed again. 'Are you still there?'

'Yes.'

'Then say something.'

'What do you expect me to say?'

'You must have some comment to make, surely.'

'I do.'

'Well?'

'Poor bugger!'

'David is an extremely nice man.'

'You'll soon put a stop to that.'

'Why must you be so disagreeable?'

'I take my cue from you, Rosemary.'

She inhaled deeply through her nose. I could see her at the other end of the line, putting a hand on her hip as she drew herself up to her full height, pursing her lips in righteous indignation. More ice was added to the cocktail. It rattled in the glass.

'I realise that this has come as a shock to you,' she said with effortless condescension. 'Coping with change was never your strong point. In fact, I can't actually remember what was. David asked me why I married you in the first place and, I must say, I'm hard put to it to come up with an answer. I mean, it's not as if it was a case of adolescent infatuation.'

'Nobody could accuse you of that!'

'You're being sarcastic again.'

'More provocation.'

'Why are you so piqued?'

'I'm not,' I lied. 'You're a big girl now, Rosemary. Free, white and over twenty-one. There's nothing to stop you getting married twice a week if you develop a taste for it. I've got no axe to grind. It lets me right out.'

Rosemary swung the mallet against my eardrum.

'I need to see you, Alan.'

'No!'

'It's imperative.'

'Why?'

'Because there's so much to discuss.'

'Talk it over with David.'

'We must make decisions.'

'You've made the only one that matters,' I said tartly. 'It's happened at last. You've found another sacrificial victim for the marriage bed. How do you propose to kill this one off?'

'Alan …'

'Congratulations!'

'We must meet.'

'Why? What else needs to be decided?'

'Lots of things.'

'We've come to a fork in the road.'

'Listen to me …'

'I go this way. You and David go that way.'

'And what about Lynette?'

11

She exchanged the mallet for a sledgehammer now and she swung it with the precision of a blacksmith. My brain was a clanging anvil. I'd been so dazed by her initial announcement that I did not see all the consequences. I had simply not thought of Lynette. Remarriage would not only substantially alter my relationship with my ex-wife, it would have a profound effect on our daughter. I saw her little enough as it was and my rights of access were continually blocked and frustrated by Rosemary. With a new husband in the frame, my problems could only increase. I might lose the most precious thing in my life. It put a hoarse note in my voice.

'This must make no difference,' I insisted.

'That's why we must get together to thrash it out. This sort of thing can only be done face to face.' She softened slightly but I was not deceived. 'I don't think I'm an unreasonable woman and I'm sure that we can come to a compromise somehow. All that it requires is a little patience and good will on both sides.'

'Yes – yours and David's.'

'Lynette will have a new father.'

'Not while the old one is alive and kicking!'

'It will have to be Friday.'

'Out of the question.'

'I've already reserved a table for lunch.'

'Thanks for consulting me first!'

'Now don't be difficult, Alan.'

'Well, I know it may seem churlish of me but I do like to have a say in my eating arrangements ... As it happens, I've done just that. I'm having lunch with someone else on Friday.'

'Cancel it.'

'Not a chance.'

'This takes precedence.'

'We'll talk through our lawyers. It may be slower that

way but it's a damned sight less painful.'

'Be there at one o'clock.'

'Sorry.'

'The Dog and Doublet.'

'Rosemary, I'm lunching with a publisher in London. Even if I wanted to – which I don't – there is no way that I can get out of it.' I heard what she said and blinked in astonishment. 'The Dog and Doublet?'

'One o'clock.'

'In Sissinghurst?'

'Of course.'

'That's cruel!' I protested. 'Positively sadistic!'

'It's convenient.'

'No, Rosemary. I draw the line at that.'

'We'll be waiting for you.'

'Then you'll wait in vain.' A pause. 'We?'

'Lynette must be in on this,' she said, playing her trump card with a ladylike flourish. 'It affects her whole future. Even you must concede that. We have to get together as a family once more – for the last time. I'm sure you'll be able to find the Dog and Doublet.'

'Don't bank on it.'

'Oh, by the way,' she said, grudgingly. 'Message for you from Lynette.'

'Well?'

'She sends her love. Goodbye.'

The line went dead but Rosemary's voice continued to buzz around inside my skull like an irate swarm of bees. All my resistance had been swept aside. I knew that I would do exactly as she ordered even though the prospect was quite terrifying. To see Lynette was usually an occasion of pure joy for me but to meet her in those circumstances would be an absolute ordeal. Rosemary had chosen the ideal venue for my humiliation.

The Dog and Doublet in Sissinghurst.

It was where I proposed to her.

Carnoustie is my only true home and I have no complaint about the warmth of her hospitality but there are times when a motor caravan is just not big enough to contain my whirling emotions. This was one such time. Rosemary had turned the place into a prison. Needing space and fresh air and the illusion of freedom, I let myself out of the vehicle and set off at a steady jog. It was only when I was halfway across the field that I realised I was holding the VAT return in my hand. Vengeance stirred. Giving way to a rare destructive impulse, I tore the form into pieces and threw them into the air to create an impromptu snowstorm.

It was an absurd gesture but it gave me satisfaction.

There could be awkward repercussions.

I didn't care.

The building was in one of those dirty, narrow backstreets in Soho that have become a wheel-clamper's paradise. Cars and vans littered both kerbs or mounted the pavements at crazy angles like mating tortoises. A couple of bicycles were chained to a lamppost. Someone had been spectacularly sick outside the pub. An empty pram was standing incongruously outside the sex shop. Refuse bins awaited collection. Piles of empty cardboard boxes completed the obstacle course. A stray dog sniffed its way along the wall to check if anyone had left a message on one of its answerphones. Pedestrians ambled along in the light drizzle. It was a depressing sight and only added to my feeling of despair.

I went up a short flight of steps and in through some double doors. After the filth and decay outside, I was plunged into hygienic modernity. Thick carpets, plain walls, gleaming leather upholstery. Reception was staffed by three well-dressed young women with competing hairstyles. My name meant nothing to the brunette with the plaits and she passed it on over the intercom with calm indifference. I was waved to a seat where I picked up a glossy catalogue of forthcoming publications. None of them aroused my interest, let alone the desire to buy them. How on earth did authors come to choose such weird subjects? I was still wondering who would want to read a book about a disused railway line in the Forest of Dean when a pert blonde came bobbing up to me.

'Mr Saxon?'

'I think so.'

'Follow me, please.'

I hauled myself out of the chair and went across to a small lift with her. In the confined space, her perfume was quite overwhelming. We rode up four floors then came out into a large area that had been divided up into offices by a series of screens. Most of the desks were occupied by Sloaney females, poring over art-work or leafing through manuscripts or engaged in nasal conversations on the telephone. Some of them recognised me from the sports pages and I got the usual mixture of curious stares and welcoming smiles.

My guide took me to the far end and opened the door of a glass-walled inner office. Its occupant leapt up from his swivel chair.

'Alan, dear chap! Come on in!'

'Thanks.'

'Nice to meet you at last.'

Harvey Jansen belonged to the Firm Handshake Brigade and he had that look-you-straight-in-the-eye technique so beloved of insurance salesmen. In my weakened state, I found it unnerving.

'You're even taller than I imagined,' he said.

'Am I?'

15

'And your hair really is grey.'

'I worry a lot.'

'On the telly, it looks silver.'

'Does it?'

'The camera doesn't do you any favours, Alan. Makes you seem much older.'

'A cunning ruse to fool the opposition.'

'It obviously works.'

'Sorry about having to cancel lunch,' I said.

'These things happen,' he said amiably. 'Main thing is that we meet before you jet off Down Under. I'm very anxious to get something down on paper.' He indicated the chair in front of the desk. 'Take a pew.' I sat down. 'What would you like – tea, coffee, hot chocolate?'

'Coffee, please.'

'How do you take it?'

'Touch of milk. No sugar.'

'Hear that, Sandra?'

He grinned at his secretary and she went off to organise the refreshments. Her perfume still teased my nostrils. Jansen chuckled.

'Sandra prides herself on her fragrance.'

'Asphyxiation at five paces.'

'You get used to it.'

Harvey Jansen beamed down at me then perched on the edge of the desk. He was a big, sleek man in a blazer and flannels with a club tie. Years older than me, he was in remarkably good condition with a healthy complexion and no excess weight. Jansen was a former rowing blue from Cambridge and he still looked as if he could pull an oar. His blend of education and physique was intimidating.

'I do hope we can work together, Alan.'

'So do I.'

'We already have a number of golf titles on our list but there's always room for something special.'

'Good.'

'*Alan Saxon on Golf*. A subtle blend of instruction, anecdote and autobiography. With lavish illustrations. All we have to do is to package it properly and it could really take off.' He sounded a warning note. 'Not that it's going to make a fortune for either of us, mark you. Sporting books don't often turn out to be overnight sensations, I fear. More a case of steady sales geared to a promotional drive.' He gave a wry smile. 'Of course, the ideal time to launch you would have been in the autumn, immediately after you'd won the Open. That would've given the book lift-off.'

'We're several years too late for that.'

'No matter,' he said breezily. 'We'll market you as the elder statesman of British golf, as the mature voice of the game. There's no substitute for experience in any sport.'

'Except luck.'

He laughed with masculine heartiness then opened his door wider when he saw the blond head bobbing towards him. His secretary brought the two cups in on a tray. She handed me my coffee, gave him his tea, then took her fragrance away again. Jansen shut the door before sitting down behind his desk. I got my first uninterrupted view of the office. It was small but impeccably tidy. Books lined three walls and I ran my eye over some of the titles.

'If there's anything you want, let me know,' he invited. 'You can have it with my compliments.'

'Thanks.'

'Might even have an advance copy of Clive's book.'

'*Fifty Famous Golfers?*'

'That's it. You get in as number fifty.'

'I hope they're in ascending order.'

'What else?' Another hearty laugh. 'Clive's a great fan of yours. It was he who suggested we got together.'

17

'Best golf writer in the business.'

'When he's sober.'

'Quite the reverse,' I said. 'It's the drink that puts him in a league of his own. It liberates him. Clive says that it makes his creative juices flow. And it doesn't seem to get in the way of his game either. He can play a mean round of golf when he's had a few.'

'So I hear.' He sipped his tea. 'I'm glad you have such a high opinion of Clive Phelps. I don't suppose you'd consider letting him write this book with you?'

'No,' I said firmly.

'He thought you wouldn't.'

'If you want my story, Mr Jansen —'

'We do, we do.'

'Then you get it in my own words.'

'I'll settle for that.'

Jansen had some more tea then set his cup aside so that he could lean forward across his desk with his hands clasped together in front of him. Having established eye contact again, he launched into what was evidently a well-prepared lecture.

'Let me give you my thoughts on this, Alan ...'

His arguments were intelligent, lucid and highly persuasive but they still could not hold my attention for more than a few minutes. Someone else had come into the office with us. Rosemary. Though I was held prisoner by his hypnotic gaze, all I could see was her. It was not Jansen's fault. If we had met for lunch as planned on the following day, we would have got on extremely well and hammered out the format of my book over a bottle of Chablis in L'Escargot. Rosemary had sabotaged all that.

Instead of having a serious discussion with my publisher, I was only half-listening to him and throwing in the occasional nod of agreement. My mind was really focused on the news about Rosemary's second marriage. Who was this David and how did she meet him? Had he been married before? What sort of stepfather would he make for Lynette? Would he have any respect for my position?

How much had she told him about me?

'Well, that more or less wraps it up, Alan.'

'Mm?'

'Did I send you to sleep?'

'No, no, Mr Jansen. It was fascinating.'

'So what's the verdict?'

'Broadly speaking ... I agree.'

'Even about the author tour?'

'Of course.'

I had no idea what I was letting myself in for but my acquiescence pleased him. He rubbed his hands together then sat back in his chair and swivelled to and fro. A thought struck him.

'Oh, by the way, you may have seen some rumours in the press about a possible takeover of HJB.' His chuckle was meant to reassure. 'Pay no attention to them. It's only sabre-rattling. Harvey Jansen Books will survive. And even if the parent company were to be taken over, we'd still preserve our editorial independence. You have no cause for concern. Either way, this book will go ahead.'

'Glad to hear it.'

'I'll draw up the contract for signature when you get back from Australia.'

'Suits me.'

'Splendid!'

He stood to signal that the interview was over. I had to endure another crushing handshake. While he went off to find me a copy of *Fifty Famous Golfers*, I browsed along the shelves and took my pick of the HJB imprint.

I settled on books about squash and cricket, the only other two sports at which I've ever shown any prowess.

Jansen came striding back with a handsomely-produced volume under his arm.

'Get Clive Phelps to sign it for you,' he said.

'I wouldn't be able to stop him.'

'Probably not.'

We shared a smile then he conducted me out. I stole a last glance at his office. Everything was so firmly in its place. A sense of order was paramount. Harvey Jansen was a man who had his life completely under control. It made me rue the chaos of my own existence even more.

How did I let myself get into such a mess?

'Let's walk down, shall we?' he said.

'Sure.'

'I need the exercise. Cooped up in there.'

We descended the steps side by side. Now that we had finished our business discussion, his manner became more confidential. There was the hint of a sigh.

'Actually, your call was a godsend.'

'Was it?'

'Lets me off the hook slightly.'

'Oh?'

'My eldest son is playing with the school orchestra tomorrow afternoon. Violin solo. His début. I'd promised to go if at all possible but our lunch date put a stop to that. Now I'll be able to sneak off and support him.'

'What school is he at?'

'Marlborough. Do you have kids?'

'Just one. A daughter.'

'You're lucky,' he said. 'I've got six.'

'By choice?'

'More by accident than design. Two from my first marriage, three I inherited from my second wife and a baby boy of our own. It makes for all kinds of complications, I can tell you, not least because my two eldest live with their mother who insists on waging a war of attrition. One long saga of divided loyalties. The recurring problem of birthdays — not to mention Christmas. I do everything on a rota system.' He put a cautionary hand on my shoulder. 'Keep it simple, Alan. You'll save yourself a lot of headaches, believe me.'

I warmed to Harvey Jansen. I'd been far too ready to take him at face value and pigeon-hole him as an educated hearty. In fact, he was not all firm handshake and piercing gaze. A degree from Cambridge had not saved him from marital disaster. Here was someone who knew all about the pangs of domestic suffering.

He had his own Rosemary.

I got the feeling that I might actually enjoy writing a book for him. Though we were poles apart in just about every respect, we had a bond. It was an unexpected comfort. On a dull afternoon in central London, he had done something I would not have thought possible.

He'd cheered me up.

It was a small victory.

Sissinghurst is a long streak of history in deepest Kent with many of the old white-painted weather-board houses looking much as they did when first built. The village is best known for its famous manor house, Sissinghurst Castle, but it was another building that held significance for me. The Dog and Doublet. An old coaching inn which dates back to the Restoration and which had been well-maintained throughout its life. Still privately owned, it had kept much of its character and individuality and it had yet to be contaminated by muzak, fruit machines and computer games.

Carnoustie was sluggish on the drive down, as if

sharing my own doubts and reluctance. She squeezed in under the arch at the rear of the pub and rolled uncertainly across the cobbled courtyard. We parked beside a white Volvo. A quick check on the other vehicles in the car park suggested that Rosemary had not yet arrived. She favoured French cars – expensive Renaults or roomy Citroëns – and there were none in sight. I was glad. It gave me a chance to sit there while I came to terms with the place and with the vivid memories which it held for me. Only when I felt strong enough did I get out, lock the door and head for my date with destiny.

The lounge bar was fairly crowded but I saw her at once. Rosemary had taken up a position in the window and was glancing through the menu. An untouched glass of sherry stood on the table beside her. She looked stunning. The light was catching her fair hair at the perfect angle and taking years off her face. Her slim-waisted blue suit with matching shoes and handbag showed that she had lost none of her elegance. My heart missed a beat. Seeing her again in this particular setting made me conscious of how beautiful she still was.

Momentarily – to my horror – desire rustled.

Then Rosemary looked up. Her cold stare robbed me of all lustful fancy. She beckoned me over as if summoning a waiter in order to make a complaint.

'I'm glad you've come early,' she said.

'Hello, Rosemary.'

'We can have a word alone.'

'I didn't notice your car outside.'

'Don't stare at me like that, Alan.'

'I'm surprised to see you, that's all.'

'Sit down.'

'Where's Lynette?'

'Sit down. I hate people hovering.'

I obeyed instinctively. 'Isn't she joining us?'

'She'll be here directly.'

'What does she think about … all this?'

'Lynette is in favour of it,' she said briskly. 'I talked it over with her. She feels that I'm ready for a new husband and it's high time she had a real father.'

'That's unkind, Rosemary!'

'Truth often is.'

'*I'm* her real father.'

'Only in name.'

'I won't let you turn my daughter against me.'

'You don't need my help in that department.'

'What do you mean!' I protested angrily.

'Keep your voice down.'

'Explain that snide remark.'

'We'll get nowhere if we bicker.'

'Lynette is mine!'

'No, Alan – she's ours. That's the problem.'

Rosemary reached for the glass and sampled the Amontillado. She had got me exactly where she wanted me. On the defensive. While I was seething, she was calm and unruffled. It was just like being married to her all over again. I took a deep breath and excused myself. Crossing to the bar I bought myself a large bitter lemon and a few minutes to collect my thoughts. Rosemary had got there before me so that she could seize the initiative. She'd taken me unawares. I had to exercise more control. When I rejoined her at the table, I felt able to do just that.

She attacked my composure at once.

'There will have to be some changes, Alan.'

'Changes?'

'Adjustments. Compromises.'

'Oh, no,' I said warily. 'Not compromises. Your idea of a compromise is that I should do exactly what you want. You have no concept of give and take.'

'We've gone beyond that stage,' she sighed.

'So what are these changes?'

'I've written them down.'

She opened her handbag and took out a folded sheet of paper, handing it to me as if serving a writ. I opened it out and saw a typed list of twelve items. None of them could be construed as good news for me. I fell back on heavy irony.

'Wouldn't thirteen have been more appropriate?'

'Those are just the major changes.'

'Losses, you mean.'

'Improvements,' she countered.

'Well, I don't agree with any of them.'

'You will.'

'Take the first one, for instance. I will not let you deny me access to Lynette.'

'That's not what I'm proposing. You'll still be able to see her from time to time.'

'But only in your presence.'

'Supervised access.'

'Heavens above – she's my daughter!'

'Then try to act in her best interests.'

Her coolness had me on the run again. I put the sheet of paper down with a gesture of contempt and tried to assert myself.

'Where is Lynette?'

'Don't be so impatient.'

'I want to see her.'

'They'll be here any moment.'

'They?'

'She and David.'

I blenched. 'David! Why the hell is he here?'

'Because I asked him to be,' she said. 'He dropped me off here then drove on down to Benenden to pick up Lynette. You should be grateful to him for making this brief chat alone with me possible.'

'That's reason for *gratitude*?'

24

'Look, whether you like it or not, David has a stake in this discussion. He has a right to be here. Lynette agreed about that.' Her smile completely disarmed me. 'Besides, I thought you'd be interested to meet him. You always said that I'd never find another man to put up with me. David has proved you wrong.'

I was speechless. It had taken all my energy to gear myself up for a meeting with Rosemary and Lynette. The thought that David might be there had never even occurred to me. I detected Rosemary's hand once again. It was a covert act of aggression. I was fairly confident of having Lynette on my side when it came to the threatened changes on Rosemary's typed list. Not any more. David altered the balance of power. It would now be three to one. Insuperable odds.

Rosemary turned to the window as another car glided into the courtyard. She gave a complacent smile.

'Here they are.'

'Where?'

'The Jaguar.'

I peered hesitantly through the glass. The vehicle was the latest model and looked as if it had just left the showroom. When it halted silently beside Carnoustie, the contrast was embarrassing. My motor caravan suddenly began to show the defects of age. Lynette was in the passenger seat of the Jag and she seemed very subdued. She had none of the bounce and sparkle that she usually brings to meetings with her father. Even when she got out of the car and gazed across at us, her expression did not change.

David Ridger escorted her towards the building. My preconceptions about him were shattered at a stroke. He was not a bit like the Identikit picture I'd created in my mind. He was much shorter and far older than I'd imagined. His hair was thinning fast, his face was quite anonymous, he walked with a slight stoop. He did not look like the owner of a brand new Jaguar. As a man, he was singularly uneventful. Rosemary had chosen as her second husband someone whose physical attributes were the opposite of my own.

Spider Woman was marrying the Invisible Man.

When they came into the lounge bar, David hung back so that Lynette could greet us first. She gave her mother a peck on the cheek then turned to me. As a rule, I get an impulsive hug that is worth driving a hundred miles for but something was clearly holding her back now.

'Hello, Daddy.'

'Hi.'

'Great to see you again.'

I had to settle for a peck on the cheek as well. If this was what supervised access meant, then it would never get my vote. Rosemary moved in to perform introductions. David Ridger gave me a limp handshake and muttered a few words. He seemed totally innocuous at close quarters and I wondered what on earth attracted Rosemary to him. She took control with characteristic ease and shunted us through into the restaurant. I was pleased to sit next to Lynette, especially when she gave my hand an affectionate squeeze under the table. Rosemary and David sat opposite us. They made an unlikely couple.

Lynette was full of news about Benenden. She had got a part in the school play, scored a goal in a hockey match and spoken in a debate on blood sports. I listened with interest and was profoundly grateful. Her excited babble was getting over those first awkward minutes. Lynette was fourteen now and beginning to resemble her mother more and more. I searched in her face and manner and gestures for the faintest hint of me. There was none.

Rosemary soon hijacked the conversation. As a

former head girl at Benenden, she was able to pull rank on Lynette and to talk expansively about how things had been in her day. She waxed lyrical about the virtues of the school and implied that its training had fitted her for a higher calling than marriage to an erratic golfing star.

Rosemary had clearly had a wonderful time at Benenden and I was forcibly reminded of my own unhappy schooldays at a Leicester comprehensive.

How had we ever got together?

The Dog and Doublet was to blame for that.

A waiter arrived and Rosemary more or less bullied us into having what she wanted us to eat. I was peeved when the wine list was handed to David as if he were the host. I tried to undermine him.

'By the way, this is on me.'

'Don't be silly,' said Rosemary.

'I insist.'

'David will pay.'

'I wouldn't hear of it.'

'The table was booked in his name.'

'Thanks for telling me!'

'Stop making a scene.'

'I want to pay the bill, Rosemary.'

'We'll discuss this later.'

'There's a principle at stake here.'

'Rubbish!'

'Alan is quite right,' said David. 'You must try to see it from his viewpoint, Rosemary. He's summoned to a vital conference with his ex-wife and daughter and he finds he's here as the guest of a complete stranger. I sympathise with him.' He turned to me. 'I really must apologise. This was not my idea.'

It was surprising enough to get such support from him but there was a bigger shock to come. Rosemary backed off. Instead of challenging him and beating

27

him down, she accepted his comments and nodded in agreement. David Ridger's quiet, cultured voice had a strong influence. He handed me the wine list.

'Why don't you choose?' he suggested politely. 'I'm sure you know far more about wine than I do.'

'Thanks.'

I studied him for a second and wondered if his self-effacing manner was simply a form of disguise. Who was the man and what did he do for a living?

Lynette answered the second part of the question.

'David's a consultant psychiatrist.'

'Is he?'

'It's a fascinating job,' she said helpfully. 'He's been telling me about it. I think he ought to take on some of our staff. They're as nutty as fruitcakes. Miss Pomeroy's a manic depressive, Hilary Turner is a schizophrenic and old Lezzie Leadbetter is a sadist.'

'Thanks, Lynette,' said David pleasantly, 'but my case-list is long enough as it is. Besides, the problems of a school like Benenden are beyond my scope, I fear. They're inherent in the fact of single sex education.'

'Boys would spoil everything,' argued Lynette.

'Psychologically, co-education is far healthier.'

If I had said that, Rosemary would have dropped on me like a ton of bricks but she raised no protest here. She deferred once again to his judgement. A thought began to flicker at the back of my mind.

Had she had a professional relationship with David? Was that how they had met?

Lynette swung the conversation in another direction.

'When are you off to Australia, Daddy?'

'Monday.'

'Wish I could come with you!'

'So do I.'

'Will you send me a post card?'

'Dozens.'

'And bring me back a boomerang? I'd love that.'

'Of course.'

'Are you going all that way just to play golf?' said David. 'Seems a strange thing to do.'

'It is,' I agreed. 'We're a strange species.'

'Where are you going?'

'Sydney, Adelaide, Melbourne.'

'Do you like Australia?'

'Very much.'

'Why?'

'Been a lucky place for me.'

'Rosemary tells me you took her there once.'

'It was hateful,' she said with disdain. 'All those dreadful people with their dreadful accents. They're so graceless. Australia likes to think of itself as modern and progressive but that's just not true. They're ridiculously provincial and old-fashioned. As for their notion of taste – well, just look at the Sydney Opera House! It's obscene. No, Australia is unspeakable. Apart from anything else, it's the world capital of male chauvinism. I loathed the whole trip.'

'That's not how I remember it,' I said.

'It was an ordeal from start to finish.'

Rosemary aimed the sentence at me like a spear and it sunk in deep. Our holiday in Australia was one of the happiest times we ever spent together. It was a second honeymoon to celebrate my winning of the British Open at Carnoustie. For once in her life, Rosemary had surrendered to the experience and revelled in it. We were never closer than during those three long, luscious weeks when she was somehow able to shed her inhibitions at last, to forget that she was a former head girl of Benenden and to commit herself totally to me and to our marriage. To hear her repudiate all that now was very painful.

The first course arrived. I had no stomach for the

food or for further argument and so I ate little and remained largely silent. Rosemary pushed various conversational topics around, Lynette chattered to hide her discomfort and David was wise and watchful. As the meal progressed, he and Rosemary began to look more and more like a couple. I'd proposed to her in a drunken moment at a table in the corner. We stayed the night at the Dog and Doublet. It increased my overdraft alarmingly but did wonders for my ego.

I now found myself asking where David had popped the question. Over a meal? During a consultation? At the wheel of his new Jaguar? I refused to believe that the great moment took place – God forbid! – in bed. Whatever else Rosemary was choosing him for, it could not be his sexual prowess. And yet, presumably, they must have slept together by now if only out of curiosity. I immediately censored the mental picture that came into my mind.

Rosemary decided that it was time the men were left alone for a while. She stage managed it with aplomb.

'Come along, Lynette.'

'Where?'

'To the Ladies' Room.'

'But I don't need to go, Mummy.'

'I think you do, darling.'

'Why?'

'This way.'

Lynette was whisked away from the table before she could say another word. David watched with amusement. Now that I was on my own with him, I felt distinctly uneasy. All at once he became a more positive and formidable human being. I was at a disadvantage. I knew very little about David Ridger but he knew a great deal about me. He started to probe.

'Is that Carnoustie outside?'

'Yes.'

'Why do you live in a motor caravan?'

'I like it.'

'Isn't it rather small?'

'That's the attraction. Back to the womb.'

'But you're such a tall man, Alan.'

'So?'

'You can't even stand up straight in that vehicle.'

'It's not a vehicle,' I corrected. 'It's a home.'

'Why live in such cramped conditions?'

'Because it's not space that I need, David. It's privacy. Carnoustie gives me that every time. She makes me feel private in the middle of a traffic jam.'

'Do you need somewhere to hide, then?'

'Oh, yes.'

'From what?'

'Wait till you've been married to Rosemary!'

He laughed but it was only to humour me. His steady gaze was unsettling. All my insecurities were set off. The last thing I wanted was for him to stroll around inside my head to make an inventory of my shortcomings.

'You're an introvert, aren't you?' he said.

'I've been called worse.'

'Curious phenomenon.'

'In what way?'

'Yours is such an extrovert profession. Golfers play in the full glare of publicity. You must rub shoulders with the mass media every time you play in a tournament.'

'I've learned to isolate myself.'

'How?'

'Years of practice.'

'What's the secret?'

'Are you charging for this consultation?'

'Sorry.' He was mildly offended. 'Let's turn to more pressing concerns. We have to discuss money.'

'I'm picking up the tab for the meal.'

'Please yourself. I was talking about Lynette.'

'Lynette?'

'If I marry her mother, your financial commitment will virtually disappear. No more child-support to pay and no more school fees.'

'But I want to pay the school fees.'

'That's not what Rosemary says.'

'Don't listen to everything she tells you.'

'Apparently, you always complain like mad.'

'Who doesn't? Those fees are exorbitant.'

'Then I'll relieve you of them, Alan.'

'They're my responsibility,' I said, 'and I accept it willingly. You're free to marry Rosemary but you are not going to buy Lynette off me!'

'That was never my intention.'

'As long as we both understand that.'

'Must you be so obstructive?'

'Force of habit.'

'So I observed.'

'I hope that concludes our discussion of money.'

'You're not the most flexible man, are you?'

'Fortunately, no.'

'How long have you suffered from tunnel vision?'

'Since the start of this conversation.'

'Rosemary warned me about you.'

'Then let me warn you about *her*.'

'I thought we could sort it all out man to man.'

'No deal.'

'Why not?'

'Because you're far too reasonable.'

He was still trying to work out what I meant when the others returned to the table. Rosemary read the look in David's eye and clicked her tongue in irritation.

'Time to go,' she announced.

'Goodbye,' I said.

'You'll have to bow to changed circumstance, Alan.'

'We'll see.'

'Thank you for coming, anyway.'

'Did I have a choice?'

'No.' She turned to Lynette. 'We'll go out to the car, darling. Since your father is determined to pay the bill, why don't you wait with him?'

Rosemary turned on her heel and stalked out with David in close pursuit. If he was going to be her husband, he would need to sharpen up on his speedy exits from public places because she had a weakness for them. Our meeting had been fairly inconclusive but I had at least turned up to face the insults. By way of a concession, Rosemary had given me a few snatched minutes with our daughter. It made all the upset worthwhile.

Lynette giggled and gave me a proper hug.

'What do you think of him?' she asked.

'David? A bit creepy.'

'He's very nice when you get to know him.'

'That's what I'm afraid of, Lynette.'

She giggled again. The waiter brought the bill and I put my Access card on his plate. He withdrew. Lynette was now looking uncannily like her mother. In the early days, Rosemary had smiled at me like that.

'Good luck in Australia!'

'Thanks.'

'Everybody who's been there says it's a fab place. Except Mummy, of course, but that's just her. She'll never admit that she enjoys anything. It's sad, really.'

'How did she come to meet David?'

'At some party or other. A charity do.'

'What does she see in him?'

'He's reliable.'

'Fair comment.'

'Oh, that wasn't meant as a dig at you, Daddy,' she said, grabbing me by the arm. 'You're the only father I want and nobody will ever replace you. But Mummy has her feelings, too. She was starting to get very mouldy before David came along. He's made all the difference.'

'Has he been married before?'

'No.'

'I thought not.'

The waiter returned and I signed the counterfoil. He bowed in gratitude at the size of the tip I had left then he tore off my copy and handed over my card. Lynette and I were free to go. A new Jaguar hooted in the car park.

'That'll be Mummy!' said Lynette.

'Who else?'

'Listen … this marriage of hers …'

'Go on.'

'Don't be too worried about it.'

'I can't say I feel like celebrating.'

'It won't alter anything. Between us.'

I kissed her on the forehead and gave her a squeeze. Out in the courtyard, the Jaguar was getting impatient. The second blast on the horn was longer and louder. We drifted across towards the door.

'Do you really like him?' I said.

'Sort of.'

'What does that mean?'

'Well, I can't honestly say that I'm mad about him or that I'd even look at someone like that for myself …'

'But?'

'There's nothing to dislike about David.'

It was an honest comment but not reassuring to me. We came out into the courtyard and had a final embrace. David held the rear door open for her and she got in. There was a flurry of goodbyes then I walked across to Carnoustie. As I got into the driver's seat, Rosemary let herself out of the Jaguar and came around for a last thrust at my self-esteem.

'You behaved appallingly,' she said.

34

'I have a tradition to keep up.'

'David was very disappointed in you.'

'As long as he doesn't try to charge me a fee.'

'Anyone can diagnose your problem, Alan,' she hissed. 'It's quite obvious that you don't have anyone at the moment. That's why this has caught you on the raw. While I've found someone to make me happy, you're still living alone in this piece of junk. I wonder why!'

She got back in the Jaguar and it drew away with impressive smoothness. I watched it in my mirror and saw Lynette waving bravely out of the rear window. It was lovely to see her again but I'd had better lunches. The parting jibe had contained too much truth for my liking. I was going through a fallow period on the emotional front and Rosemary had been quick to remind me of it. The trouble was she reminded me of something else.

How much I still loved her.

It was time to go to Australia to find out why.

CHAPTER TWO

SINGAPORE AIRPORT IS NOT MY favourite place at the best of times. It's far too big, futuristic and soulless for my liking. Thousands upon thousands of transit passengers are processed each day on an endless human conveyor belt. Individualism is out. It is strictly a numbers operation. When I got my first sight of the building through bleary and half-closed eyes, I groaned inwardly. Its brightness dazzled me. I was made to pay heavily for my stupidity on the flight out.

Having brooded about Rosemary until we were halfway across Europe, I tried to drown my sorrows in the time-honoured way. Normally, I rarely touch alcohol when I fly and rely on orange juice to combat dehydration. This time it was different. Several stiff whiskies slipped down with ease and helped me to keep self-pity at bay. Too much wine with too little food compounded the folly. I fell into a stupor, slept throughout the film that was shown, and had to be shaken awake when we landed. As I blundered off the aircraft with a championship hangover, I walked into a solid wall of light and sound. Dropping down on to the nearest seat, I wanted simply to be left alone so that I could fade away quietly into oblivion.

Fate did not grant me my last wish.

'Saxon, you old devil! You made it at last!'

'Oh God!'

'Welcome to sunny Singapore!'

'Lower your voice, Clive.'

'Aren't you pleased to see me?'

'No.'

'Ungrateful turd!'

'I'm dying.'

'Good.'

'Show some respect.'

'I'll dance on your bloody grave.'

He knelt down so that he could study me more closely. Diagnosing the symptoms at once, he let out a peel of callous laughter and blew cigar smoke over me. Clive Phelps is a loyal friend and a brilliant golf writer but he has no sympathy for a man who cannot hold his drink. My predicament only amused him.

'You look terrible,' he said gleefully.

'Shut up.'

'My grandmother has more colour in her cheeks than you and they buried her three years ago. You look as if you've just swum ten lengths in a whisky distillery with your mouth wide open. Well, this really is a turn-up for the book! Alan Saxon, pissed as a fart. What happened? Did somebody spike your orange juice?'

'I need help.'

'Booze is for real boozers, old son.'

'Now he tells me!'

'Stick to golf.'

I tried to formulate a reply but the words just would not come and, besides, I sensed that I was now alone. I forced my eyes open but the effort was so agonising that I closed them instantly. Unable to move or speak, I had to remain slumped in my seat while I listened to the ten-pin bowling match that was being played inside my skull. My whole head vibrated as someone scored a strike. Clive came back.

'Drink this.'

'Eh?'

'Come on. Do as you're told.'

'No … please.'

'Doctor's orders.'

He held a plastic beaker to my lips and poured some of the liquid down my throat. It tasted foul and made me sit up to retch. Clive was pleased with my progress.

'See? Making you better already.'

'What in God's name is it?'

'Hair of the dog. Open up.'

'Oh no.'

'Take your medicine.'

'Not again.'

'You must,' he said, forcing me to take another mouthful. 'It's great stuff. I know it tastes like last Friday's camel piss but it works wonders. Just trust me.'

I was too weak to resist and I let him empty the beaker. The drink burned my throat and smouldered in my stomach for a while. Then the miracle happened. Very slowly, my brain began to clear. The bowling match inside my skull was abandoned and my eyes no longer felt like giant ball-bearings that were straining to get free of their sockets. I still felt rocky but hope had now been restored. There was an outside chance that I might live.

When I parted my lids, the pain was only minimal. I saw the ravaged face of Clive Phelps, topped by a wild outcrop of curly hair and polished to a light brown sheen by a few days in the sun. A triumphant smile peeped out from beneath his bushy moustache.

'What do you say to me?' he demanded.

'Put that cigar out.'

'Don't I get any thanks?'

'The jury's not in yet.'

'Why do I bother!'

'Rewards of the heart.'

'Balls!'

He burst out laughing again then sat down beside me to put a fraternal arm around my shoulders. I was feeling better with every second. His ebullience was no longer a bombing raid on my sensibilities. I was glad to see him.

'Serves you right, Saxon!' he said.

'Does it?'

'You would try to get to Oz in one go. Fatal. Enough to drive anyone to drink. Take a leaf from my book. Do it in stages. I had a weekend in Dubai, playing golf on that amazing course that has to be watered every twenty-four hours. Two days in Bangkok sharing myself out among the local maidenry. Then two further days here. Bliss!'

'Obviously agrees with you.'

'My idea of heaven. Until you've been to the Raffles Country Club, you haven't lived. Female umbrella caddie to keep you in the shade. Female golfing caddie to carry your clubs for you. Terrific course. What else do you need? I played a round each day and I played around each night. And they call this work!' A sordid memory produced a low snigger. 'Hey, shall I tell you what happened at the Singapore Island Club ...?'

There was no way to halt him. Clive is not just a kiss-and-tell merchant. He gives you an action-packed video of his sex life in glorious technicolour. I've never really understood his compulsion and I still can't reconcile this roving lecher with the other Clive Phelps that I know. Meet him at home and he's a doting husband and an indulgent father. He genuinely loves his family. Yet the moment he walks out of the house on another assignment, he becomes a rampant satyr with a gleam in his eye. No trip is complete without a conquest, no conquest is complete without a blow-by-blow account for his selected friends.

I heard very little of what he said and I believed even less. My ears pricked up when he turned to the reason that was taking us both to Australia.

'Oxley has pushed the boat out.'

'Has he?'

'Jackpot now stands at nearly four hundred grand.'

'Wow!'

'Chance for you to make a killing.'

'Wish there was.'

'Christ, there're only three men to beat!'

'Oh, sure,' I said. 'Trouble is they happen to be the three best players in the world. I hope to do well but I'm not superman.'

'England expects.'

'Don't oversell me, Clive.'

'Then don't undersell yourself.'

I was going to Sydney by invitation to play in a Skins Game. It was being sponsored by Warren Oxley, one of the new breed of Australian multi-millionaires who seem to make a success of anything they get their hands on. Four of us were to pit ourselves against each other over thirty-six holes of golf. The prize money was highly enticing but Oxley was no philanthropist. He'd find a way to make a profit out of the event from television coverage, from a network of advertising deals and from money at the turnstiles. A massive hype was already under way. Warren Oxley lived in a world of superlatives.

'This is the big one,' said Clive. 'You're in.'

'Wish I could share your confidence.'

'The pot of gold is yours for the taking, Alan. If you hit form, you could romp away. I don't see anyone to trip you up.'

'Aren't you forgetting Rod Melville?'

'No.'

'Oh, come on, Clive. He's been nothing short of

41

sensational this year. Rod is top of the US Money List by a clear margin and he's left the rest of us standing in the Sony World Rankings. Okay, he's a big, brash Aussie who shoots his mouth off but he's one hell of a golfer. Two majors, four other tournament wins, six top ten finishes – the guy's on a hot streak.'

'Agreed. Rod Melville is number one right now.'

'Then how am I supposed to beat him?'

Clive gave a secret smile and stroked his moustache. He looked like a Victorian poisoner who is plotting the demise of his next victim. Evidently, he knew something.

'Answer me,' I pressed. 'Rod will be playing on his home patch with a fanatical gallery behind him. All the advantages lie with him. How do I compete with that?'

'You don't, Alan.'

'What do you mean?'

'Rod Melville has withdrawn.'

'Are you serious?'

'Got the news this morning. Rang a friend of mine at the *Sydney Morning Herald* to see what the latest betting was – it doesn't flatter you, by the way, but that will change now.'

'Why?'

'Rod Melville is out. According to my mate, the great man was involved in a car accident near Broken Bay. Quite a bad one. Fractured pelvis, cracked ribs and goodness knows what else. Broken Bay might've been named after him.' He exhaled more cigar smoke and waited until I finished coughing. 'Cross him off your worry list. Rugged Rod will not be wielding his wonder clubs for some time.'

'That's rotten luck! What exactly happened?'

'Who cares? He's gone – you move in.'

'It's not as easy as that.'

'You can handle Wexler and Limsong. They're both

good but they've got nothing like your experience in this sort of contest. A Skins Game really gets to the nerve ends. When the heat is on, they'll both start to fry.'

'Who's taking Rod Melville's place?'

'Brace yourself.'

'Oh no!'

'Sorry.'

'I knew there'd be a catch.'

'Rise above it.'

'Did it have to be Gil Jericho?'

'You can't expect Oxley to stage an event like this without an Aussie golfer in the frame. Jericho was the obvious choice. He may not be in Melville's class – who is? – but he's still a thoroughbred.' He smirked evilly. 'Also, of course, he'll stir things up.'

'Don't remind me.'

Gilbert Jericho was the man I was most pleased to avoid on the professional golf circuit. That being the case, Sod's Law decreed that we should be thrown together as often as possible. The kindest description of our relationship was that we did not hit it off. There were many reasons and I did my best to forget them. It was now eighteen months since Jericho and I were partnered on a golf course. The period had been one of merciful release.

I'd been really looking forward to the Skins Game. Herm Wexler was to fly the American flag. Sam Limsong would represent Thailand with distinction. I was the British interest and Rod Melville was the Australian megastar. Four continents would be ranged against each other. It was a privilege to be in such company.

Until the name of Gil Jericho intruded.

I wanted to jump on the next plane home.

'Don't let him get to you,' advised Clive.

'Tell me how.'

'Borrow my trumpet.'

'What are you on about?'

'Christianity, you ignoramus.'

'Speak in English.'

'Jericho. Trumpets. Walls tumbling down.' He rolled his eyes in disgust. 'Holy shit! Don't you ever read the Gideon Bible in your hotel bedroom?'

'Not very often. Neither do you.'

'That's because I'm always otherwise engaged.'

'I'm beginning to wish that I was!'

'Everything will be fine, Alan.'

'Why? Is some guardian angel going to arrange a car accident for Gil Jericho as well?'

'Funny you should mention that.'

'Eh?'

'That's my other bit of news.'

'What is?'

'Rod Melville's prang near Broken Bay.'

'Well?'

'It was no accident.'

Although I'd never actually met Warren Oxley, I reserved the right to dislike him for what he was and for the complex machinations that got him there. If the world had more people like me in it and less like him then it would be a far saner and healthier place. Power and influence are fearsome weapons when they're in the wrong hands and my guess was that Oxley's hands were as wrong as they come. Notwithstanding all this, I spared him a sigh of gratitude when I set foot on Australian soil. Not only did he use those wrong hands to pull strings that speeded my progress through Customs, he had a chauffeur-driven Mercedes waiting to spirit me away to my hotel. After a total journey lasting twenty-three hours, this kind of treatment is the ideal balm. With unashamed pleasure, I stood in the middle of the arrivals lounge and savoured Warren Oxley's millions. He'd bought my approval.

Clive Phelps thumbed a lift and the uniformed chauffeur was not at all put out to be driving a lanky Pom golfer in a track suit and a dissipated journalist in flower shirt and shorts that were covered in cigar ash. Stranger couples had occupied his rear seats and they had not always sat politely side by side.

We dropped Clive off at the Regent then cruised on to the Hilton International in Pitt Street. A whole suite had been reserved for me on the top floor. It commanded a superb view over the city that I was not yet ready to enjoy and just about all of life's little luxuries. My bed was big enough to park Carnoustie in and the bathroom had a marble whirlpool bath. I opted for gushing hot water first and promptly fell asleep. When I awoke an hour or so later, the water was cold and lifeless. I swathed myself in warm white towels and staggered out. Sitting on the bed to dry myself, I nodded off again as jet-lag came in for a second attack. This time I surrendered completely. It was ten hours or more before I surfaced to find that I was tucked in under the bedclothes without a stitch on.

The telephone was ringing nearby. I grabbed it.

'Hello?'

'Alan Saxon?'

'Probably.'

'Welcome to Sydney. I hope the flight was not too tiring for you.'

'Ask me in a week's time.'

She had a nice laugh and a crisp telephone manner. I put her in her twenties. She sounded pleased to hear me.

'I'm Jan Cummings,' she introduced.

'Hi, Jan.'

'One of Mr Oxley's PAs. I've been in charge of organising your accommodation. Everything okay?'

'No complaints so far.'

'Let me know if there are.'

'How do I get in touch?'

'Oh, you'll be seeing a lot of me, Alan.'

'This gets better and better.'

An involuntary yawn caught me completely unawares.

'Have I woken you up?' she asked in concern.

'Not completely. Shout louder.'

'I assumed you'd be up by now.'

'When's now?'

'Ten-thirty in the morning.'

The digital clock on the bedside table confirmed the time. If anybody had to drag me out of my slumbers, I was glad it was Jan Cummings. Her brightness was refreshing though I wished she didn't have to end every sentence on a rising inflection. Vanquishing a second yawn, I sat up to make myself more comfortable. I intended to be part of this new day.

'I rang to invite you to dinner this evening at Mr Oxley's home in Point Piper. It's a small private party to give you the chance to meet everybody. The others will be there as well.'

'Others?'

'Herm Wexler has been in Sydney for a week now. He wanted to get in plenty of practice on the course. Sam Limsong arrived two days ago.'

I tensed. 'What about Gil Jericho?'

'How did you know he was taking part?'

'Instinct.'

'Word travels fast,' she said. 'Gil has stepped into the breach at the last moment so he still has other commitments to honour. He's up in Queensland right now and won't be able to join us until Thursday.'

46

'Does that mean he'll miss tonight's party?'

'Unfortunately, yes.'

'In that case, I'll be there.'

'Good. A car will pick you up at seven.'

'Thanks, Jan. You're working well.'

'Look forward to meeting you, Alan.'

'Same here. Oh, one last thing ...'

'Yes?'

'Warren Oxley. I've heard so many conflicting stories about him. Between you, me and the jacuzzi, what's your esteemed employer really like?'

'Is this a serious question?'

'Deadly serious.'

It made her consider her answer very carefully.

'He's a most exceptional man.'

'In what way?'

'You'll find out.'

It's amazing how quickly a day can drift past when you are trying to adjust to a new time zone. Before I knew what was happening, it was late afternoon and I was stirring from another doze. All that I'd managed to do was to have a shower, get dressed, go down for brunch and buy a few post cards and a morning paper in the hotel shop. My urge to write to Lynette was smothered by my memories of the meal at the Dog and Doublet. I needed more time to recover and to adapt to the fact that Rosemary was going out of my life in a more complete and lasting way. I would have to learn a new language in which to converse with my daughter.

Restored and invigorated by the whirlpool bath, I turned to a chore that is usually high on my list when I travel abroad. I reached for my golf bag and inspected my clubs. Baggage handlers at airports are not the most gentle and considerate human beings and I have more than once had a nasty shock when I examined my clubs after long flights. This time the damage was very minor – scuff marks on the bag itself and a slight tear in one of the hoods. The tools of my trade were in good condition. Australia was once again proving to be a lucky place for me.

Then I remembered Gil Jericho.

That sent me to the sports pages of the paper which had a big article about the forthcoming Skins Game. We were all shown in action photographs. Mine was taken at the Australian Open back in 1983. The tournament was held at Kingston Heath, a fine course that's laid out on sandy heathland in the suburbs of Melbourne. The camera caught me on the tee at the sixth hole – the toughest on the course in my view – putting every ounce of energy into a towering drive. What the picture did not reveal was the lurking figure of Gil Jericho to my right. During our stroll up the last fairway, I threatened to punch him if he resorted to any more of his sly tricks. My anger was put to good effect in that tee shot.

The article did not dwell on Rod Melville's fate. No mention of the car accident. No whisper of any possible sabotage. He was 'indisposed'. I made a mental note to find out which hospital he was in.

Feeling hungry again, I rang room service and had tea and sandwiches sent up. An hour raced by. It was soon time to get ready for my outing. Sydney can get very hot in November and I'd taken the precaution of bringing my white cotton suit. I've learned to ignore the fact that it makes me look like an African missionary.

My chauffeur was punctual. On the dot of seven, I got a call to say that the car had arrived. It was the driver who'd met me at the airport so I promoted myself to the front seat as a sign of friendship. He liked that.

'What about the others?' I asked.

'What others?'

'Herm Wexler and Sam Limsong.'

48

'They have their own drivers.'

'So I've got you all to myself?'

'That's right.'

His name was Vic and he was a cheerful companion. He was a burly man of middle height, close to my own age. His face looked as if it had seen the inside of a boxing ring and he gave the impression that he could still acquit himself well in a fight. An uncompromising Sydneysider, he was a mine of useless information about the city.

'There are six million rivets in the coathanger.'

'The Harbour Bridge?'

'Over six thousand vehicles an hour cross it at peak times. That's because fifty per cent of the population go to work in a car. Know how many people visited Taronga Zoo since it first opened in 1916?'

'I can't wait to find out, Vic.'

His statistical survey of his birthplace got us to our destination in no time. I could see that I was in for an educative experience every time he drove me but I didn't mind that. Vic was an interesting character. When the Mercedes came to a halt, he got out and came round to open my door for me. I warmed to him even more. Then I noticed something that made me revise my opinion. As he bent forward, there was a distinctive bulge under the left side of his uniform. Our relationship subtly altered.

He was carrying a gun.

Point Piper is an exclusive suburb on a finger of land that pokes out boldly into the harbour. I could rely on Warren Oxley to have a prestige address but I'd wildly overestimated the size of his house. It was much smaller and far less ostentatious than I'd envisaged. Only five bedrooms at most. The place was shrouded in foliage. I walked around to the front door.

'Alan! Come and join the party.'

'You must be Jan.'

'That's me.'

'Nice to meet you.'

I got a handshake and a smile that made me forget all about the number of visitors to the Taronga Zoo. Jan Cummings was a leggy redhead in a green silk blouse and a white pleated skirt. One glance told me it would be much more fun to count her freckles than to add up the number of rivets used in Sydney Harbour Bridge. Her eyes flirted momentarily but her manner was strictly professional.

'Follow me,' she said.

'Best offer I've had all day.'

'How's the jet-lag?'

'Improved enormously in the last five seconds.'

She gave that nice laugh of hers and opened the door to the lounge. It was large and light with floor-to-ceiling windows at the end which overlooked the water. Eight or nine people were standing around with drinks in their hands but I only saw one of them.

Warren Oxley claimed all my attention. He was a big, fleshy, handsome man with a Mediterranean cast of feature and a thick black beard that gave him an almost piratical air. He was soberly dressed in a light grey mohair suit and had a gold pin in his tie. A set of perfect teeth came into view as he gave me a handshake that would have hurt Harvey Jansen's fingers.

'Great to see you, Alan!'

'Thanks, Mr Oxley.'

'Warren, please. Don't stand on ceremony.'

'Okay. Warren.'

'So you're the Pom contingent.'

'I left my Union Jack back at the hotel.'

'Don't be afraid to wave it when you get out on the

50

course, mate,' he said jovially. 'In the metaphorical sense, that is. We must get some aggro going. Poms against the Aussies. Yanks against the Japs.'

'Sam Limsong is from Thailand.'

'Comes to the same thing.'

'Not in his book.'

Someone put a glass of white wine in my hand. I sipped it and nodded appreciatively. Oxley beamed.

'Australian Chardonnay.'

'Delicious.'

'We make the best wine in the world.'

'The French always claim that they do.'

'Sour grapes!'

He laughed at his own joke and squeezed my arm as if determined to leave a permanent set of fingerprints on it. Warren Oxley was a strong man. He exuded vitality. Behind the pirate grin and the affable manner was a sense of power that had to be carefully restrained.

'Alan Saxon,' he said thoughtfully.

'Present and correct.'

'Born in Leicester, England. May 16, 1951. Height – six foot two. Weight – a hundred and eighty-five pounds or thereabouts. Turned pro in 1972. Career highlights: Dutch Open, Spanish Open, French Open, Heritage Classic, Greater Greensboro, Suntory World Matchplay Championship, Australian PGA and so on. Not forgetting the British Open at Carnoustie, of course. Present address: motor caravan with sentimental attachment.'

'You've obviously done your homework.'

'Information is the name of the game.'

'Did you check me out on your computer?'

'Naturally. That's why you're here.'

'I'm glad I passed the test.'

'You're a wayward genius on a golf course, Alan.

Every time they write you off, you come storming back to make them eat their fucking words. You're a rebellious bastard who just won't lie down. I like that. We're two of a kind, mate. Brothers under the skin.'

I doubted it very much. Warren Oxley was nothing like the Alan Saxon that I knew. I still believed in such romantic notions as freedom and equality and doing good unto others. He was motivated by conquest.

'You had a fantastic run this year,' he said.

'It wasn't bad.'

'Then it came to a sudden halt.'

'Injury.'

'How is the wrist?'

'Didn't they have the X-rays on your computer?'

He heard the sarcastic note in my voice and leaned forward.

'Your father was a policeman, wasn't he?'

'Still is.'

'Know what mine was?'

'Minister for Information?'

My quip needled him and he fixed me with a glare.

'My father was a sponge diver. A dumb Greek immigrant who came to Darwin after the war in search of enough money to feed his wife and kids. Since nobody could pronounce his surname and teased him like mad, he changed it to Oxley. We all got English names into the bargain. Dad worked his balls off to provide for us, and where did it get him? Dived once too often and his lungs packed in. They brought him home under a tarpaulin. He was thirty-six.' He bristled. 'I grew up that day. I vowed that it wasn't going to happen to me. No matter what it took, I'd fight my way out of that kind of life.'

'You succeeded, Warren.'

'Yes,' he said with deep satisfaction. 'I did it. I can buy and sell everyone in this room ten times over.

That's what information does for you. And I'm still a year younger than when my old man died.'

'That's some achievement.'

'Remember it,' he warned.

'Can I ask you something?'

'Go ahead.'

'Do you actually like golf?'

He roared with laughter. 'It bores the fucking pants off me, Alan. I'd sooner watch paint dry but there's no money in that. Golf is death on wheels. Only one thing worse than watching it and that's having to play the bloody game. Does that answer your question?'

It did. In every respect.

Some more people came into the room and Warren Oxley ditched me expertly to greet them. I was glad to escape him before I talked myself into real trouble. He was the sort of man who could have you killed if he took against you and I'd never win prizes for diplomacy. Oxley made my hackles rise. I resented the way he had Alan Saxon carefully stored away on his computer. His research would be thorough. He probably knew what I chose from the menu at the Dog and Doublet.

I drank some more wine and recalled what Clive Phelps always said – you don't have to like someone to take his money. It was sensible advice.

Two familiar figures bore down on me.

'Hi, Al. How goes it?'

'Hello, Herm.'

'You know Mary Anne, don't you?'

'Of course.'

'Hi there,' she said.

'When d'you hit town?' he asked.

'Yesterday.'

'Mistake.'

'Why?'

53

'You shoulda worked more practice time into your schedule. I tell you, this course is a gorilla. It'll beat the shit out of you.'

Herman Wexler was very endearing. He was a complete neurotic. Anybody else with his immense natural talent would have been brimming with confidence but he was a mass of insecurities. Though he'd been a top player on the USPGA Tour for some years now, it never seemed to reassure him. He was terrified he'd lose his touch if he didn't constantly tune up his game. Herm Wexler was short, slight and balding with a frown like a series of chevrons. When they made the film of his life, they'd automatically choose Woody Allen in the title role.

'You been out to Greenblades?' he said.

'Not yet.'

'Boy, there's some eighteen holes out there!'

'As tough as Royal Sydney?'

'Tougher.'

'What about the Australian?'

'No comparison. Greenblades is a real lulu. It could get very embarrassing for all of us, believe me. A week is not enough, is it, Mary Anne?'

'If you say so, Herm.'

'I shoulda come for a fortnight. A month even.'

Looking at him now, nobody would guess that this tormented little man won the US Open by four clear shots from a quality field at no less a venue than Oakmont, that glorious stretch of flatlands near the Alleghenies which is high on any pro's list of the world's most challenging golf courses. Herm Wexler had wrestled with gorillas before and always won on a submission. It did not still his sense of panic.

'I struggled out there today.'

'Take your mind off it, honey.'

'How can you say that, Mary Anne?'

54

'This is a party.'

'But you saw me at Greenblades.'

'Relax, sweetie. Tomorrow you'll do better.'

Cursed with a nervous disposition, Herm was certainly blessed in his wife. Dark, attractive and serene, Mary Anne Wexler was his salvation. They complemented each other and beneath the apparent craziness of their lifestyle was a bedrock of love and commitment that took them past every problem, even those that Herm so assiduously created for himself.

Their togetherness made me brutally aware of the deficiencies in my own marriage. After chatting with them for a few minutes, I eased my discomfort by moving away to exchange my now empty glass for a full one. I then found a neutral corner from which I could study the guests. Over a dozen people were now in the room. The only golfers present were myself, Herm Wexler and the tall figure of Sam Limsong. The rest looked like business associates of our host, slick and sleek, created in his own image. Jan Cummings was circulating with practised ease.

Fresh air beckoned. One of the windows had been slid open to give access to the patio beyond. I drifted out to find myself alone. The view was breathtaking. You can study the harbour from a hundred different angles and it never lets you down. I'd forgotten how much solace you could draw from it. Craft of all sizes were plying their way through the gentle swell. Land curved sinuously in the distance around the edge of the water. The sun was an orange beach ball falling in slow motion towards the horizon. I was entranced.

Her voice tapped me on the shoulder.

'Alan! How nice to see you!'

'Oh.'

'I'm Diane Reinhold.'

'Hi.'

I turned to look at a tall, slim woman in a red satin blouse and a pair of black culottes. Her fair hair was cut short and brushed back from her high forehead. The face had a quiet loveliness that needed no make-up. Diane Reinhold was very pleased to see me and yet I felt an instinctive hostility towards her without knowing why.

'Good of you to come all this way,' she said.

'From the hotel?'

'From England.'

'Ah yes.'

'How's the weather there?'

'Pretty miserable.'

'Nothing changes.'

Her accent puzzled me. There was an Australian twang that was overlaid with a transatlantic drawl and softened by the occasional vowel sound from the Home Counties. She saw my bewilderment and dispelled it at once.

'New Zealand.'

'What?'

'That's where I was born and brought up. We moved to Chicago when I was ten then across to England. I did my "A" Levels in a girls' school down in Hampshire. Then it was off to Melbourne University.'

'You get around, Diane.'

'It shows in my voice.'

Perhaps it was that knowing look which was annoying me. I'd seen it on the faces of David Ridger and Warren Oxley, two people who'd broken through my privacy barrier to unsettle me in different ways. David had an insight into my marital career while Oxley had just about everything else taped. Diane was doing the same thing to me. I resented her easy familiarity.

'Who do you fear most?' she said.

'The VAT inspector.'

'I was talking about the Skins Game.'

'Oh, golf.'

'Which player will you look out for?'

'Myself.'

'You're not concerned about the others?'

'I've got enough to worry about with my own game. They can take care of themselves. If I was to let the strength of the opposition rattle me beforehand, then I'd never compete in a tournament.'

'Sensible attitude.'

Her interest seemed genuine but I still could not bring myself to like her. I glanced into the room as I heard the braying laugh of our host.

'Do you work for Warren Oxley?'

'We all do.'

'Don't you find him a bit overpowering?'

'Not really.'

'I suppose you think he's a real softie underneath.'

'I know he is.'

'Difficult to believe that.'

'What have you got against Warren?'

'It's not the man, it's the breed.'

'Aussies?'

'Millionaires. Money warps the character. I've never met a human being yet who was improved by the possession of a large amount of wealth.'

Diane smiled. 'Okay, it may not make them angels. But wealth makes a devil much more attractive. I had a feeling that you and Warren would not see eye to eye.'

'Why?'

'My knowledge of him.'

'And?'

'Your reputation.'

'For what?'

'Being the odd man out.'

'A defect of birth.'

57

'Have you always been such a boat-rocker?'

'Only when I don't trust the captain.'

She sipped her drink slowly and watched me over the rim of her glass. Diane Reinhold was at once intrigued and peeved with me. She adopted a finger-wagging tone.

'Warren's gone to a lot of trouble for you.'

'Yes. Had me checked out good and proper.'

'He's put a lot of capital into this venture.'

'Only because he expects to get lots more out.'

'What do you mean?'

'Well, let's face it. He's got no interest in golf as such. All he can see are the commercial potentialities of the game. If he could make more profit out of staging a tiddlywinks tournament, he'd be doing that instead.'

'You malign him, Alan.'

'I happen to love the game I play.'

'You're not the only one.'

'Oxley hates golf.'

'That only makes the gesture more worthwhile.'

'Gesture?'

'Towards me. There's something I should have told you at the start. I'm his wife.'

'Oh dear! Foot-in-the-mouth-time.'

'Warren didn't want to sponsor this event.'

'Then why did he?'

'Because I asked him to do it. As a favour.'

I gulped. 'All this is down to you?'

'Women can love golf as well, you know.'

'Granted. Even so …'

'Husbands like Warren Oxley don't indulge them. Is that what you think? You're wrong, Alan. When we got married six months ago, he asked me what I most wanted. I told him I'd like to have four of the best golfers in the world playing in a Skins Game. Just for me.'

'And that's why we're here?'
'Yes. This is my wedding present.'

Years of travelling around the globe has taught me a lot about my biological clock. Australia always knocks me out for the first day then gets me every morning – regardless of how late I go to bed – at six o'clock. In the old days, I used to fight it but now I have the sense to make use of it. A hot bath gave me a chance to reflect on the dinner party at Point Piper. Having been put in my place by the hostess, I spent most of the evening in resolute silence, stuck at the dining table between Jan Cummings and one of Oxley's henchmen. The meal was excellent and the conversation lively but I was preoccupied by a single thought.

Why did I find Diane Reinhold so objectionable?

She was a woman of quality and a considerate hostess. Her passion for the game of golf was as real as it was surprising. Yet I could not respond to her with any warmth. Only when I was leaving the house did I realise why. It was not just the fair hair and the upward tilt of the chin. It was not just the frightening self-assurance. It was her ability to disturb me at a very deep level.

She reminded me of Rosemary.

After a light breakfast in my room, I gathered my things together and went downstairs. Vic was waiting for me with a cheerful grin. He made no complaint about the early hour. My golf bag was put in the boot and we set off towards Sydney Harbour Bridge.

'Are you sure the club will be open?' I said.

'They'll be open.'

'And there'll be a caddie for me?'

'I arranged it last night.'

'Thanks, Vic.'

'All part of the service.'

He started to regale me with useless facts about the growth in the city's population over the past two hundred years. I gave him his head and pretended to be suitably impressed as each new statistic was reeled off by this self-appointed historian of his home town.

'More than doubled since 1947.'

'Amazing, Vic!'

'Sixty per cent of the population of New South Wales now live in Sydney.'

'Incredible.'

A dispute with a taxi driver saved me from running out of new ways to express my awe. Vic lowered the window and exchanged some ripe language with the other driver who did a lot of fist-waving but lost the argument. I took advantage of the break in the commentary to get in a few questions.

'Why Greenblades?'

'Not with you, mate.'

'Why isn't the Skins Game being held at the Royal Sydney or the Australian or the New South Wales Golf Club? They're the premier courses here. Greenblades is still relatively new and unproven. Why choose that?'

'Search me.'

'No ideas at all?'

'Not really,' he said. 'Mr Oxley's pumping some cash into the club, that's all I know. Maybe he wants to sort of protect his investment. That make sense?'

I began to get the message. Further speculation was rudely curtailed. Vic's eye had been flicking up to the rear-view mirror at regular intervals. It stayed there a little longer this time and hardened. His foot went down on the accelerator and we powered away, overtaking a stream of traffic before making a sudden right-hand turn. The chauffeur's knowledge of the city was not confined to mindless trivia. Every twist and turn of its street plan was second nature to him and he took us on a lightning tour. I glanced over my shoulder but saw nothing in pursuit. After minutes of controlled recklessness, the car slowed down and rejoined a main road.

'Are we being tailed?' I said.

'Not any more.'

'Who was it?'

'Nobody.'

We were now crossing the Harbour Bridge towards the north shore. Vic was a changed man. Being followed had upset him. He didn't mention a single rivet.

Greenblades Country Club was a twenty-minute drive through the northern suburbs. The Mercedes hugged the coast nearly all the way and I could see the stiff breeze tugging at the sails out on the water. Links courses that are at the mercy of high winds hold terrors for even the most accomplished masters of the game. As we swung off the road and followed a long tree-lined lane, I sensed that Greenblades would have additional hazards.

We drove through a pair of imposing wrought-iron gates that stood at the entrance then rolled for a hundred yards or more along a gravel path. Vic parked us in the car park at the rear of the clubhouse. It was a long, low, ugly building of redbrick and pantiles and yet money had clearly been lavished on it. I hoped that Oxley's proposed extension could somehow redeem the place as a piece of architecture. There was nobody about and no sign of any other vehicle. We got out and went around to the boot to collect my golf bag.

'The place is deserted, Vic.'

'Someone opened the gates for us.'

'It's only just eight o'clock.'

'We have early risers in Sydney.'

Before he could give me statistics on the subject, I took my bag and sauntered around to the front of the clubhouse. It looked much more appealing from this perspective. There was a wide verandah with an ornate wooden balustrade along it. Members could relax with their drinks in cane chairs and watch games reaching their climax on the nearby eighteenth green. If the weather were inclement, they could stay in the bar and view the action on the course through the picture windows. Greenblades was improving the more I studied it.

'Locker room here,' said Vic, pointing to a door.

'What if it's closed?'

'It won't be.'

His confidence was justified. I paused halfway in.

'Where's my caddie?'

'All under control.'

'Is he inside?'

'Just get ready.'

I took his advice and went through into the kind of locker room that makes you drool. No expense had been spared. It was large, luxurious and superbly equipped. Showers, sauna and a whirlpool bath awaited returning players. Locker space was generous and the toilets were a work of art. The shortcomings of the exterior were more than counter-balanced. There was something else that I liked about the Greenblades locker room. Despite its newness and its faint smell of disinfectant, it had an authentic atmosphere. Hundreds of minor dramas had already been enacted within its gleaming walls. Winners had boasted here and losers had suffered the slings and arrows of outrageous fortune. The place was steeped in joy and despair. It was a real golf club.

I changed quickly and examined myself in a full-length mirror. The sun was warm but that wind insisted on a Pringle sweater. I wore blue trousers and white shoes. A tartan cap and a black glove completed the outfit. I did a few exercises to limber up then swung my bag on to my shoulder and went out again.

My caddie was waiting for me with a smile.

'Gidday, Alan.'

'What are you doing here?'

'Waiting for you.'

'There must be some mistake. Where's Vic?'

'Gone back to the car.'

'He promised to arrange things.'

'Have you never had a female caddie before?'

Diane Reinhold wore sweater, slacks and a sun visor with the name of the club on it. She was fit, alert and raring to go. I, by contrast, no longer had the same eagerness to get out on the course. It was the Rosemary Syndrome all over again. I'd been set up.

'Shall we go, Alan?'

'I'm not sure I like this at all.'

'But I know Greenblades backwards.'

'You also happen to be the wife of the sponsor.'

'So? What's your worry? Think the others will complain that you got inside help? They've had their share. I've spent hours talking about the course to Herm Wexler and to Sam Limsong. I told you. I'm a golf freak.'

'What I need is a caddie,' I said pointedly.

Her buoyant charm faded for a second but she soon turned it on again. I was treated to a big smile.

'Let me make a bargain with you,' she said.

'I'm listening.'

'Give me a chance for the first three holes.'

'No point, Diane.'

'Please. Bear with me. I'll be your caddie for three holes and do my damnedest to break down your stupid male prejudices. If you still decide I'm not up to it, I'll

63

quit there and then and send out someone else to take my place. Is that fair?'

'No.'

'Why not?'

'Look, it's nothing personal ...'

'Well, it sounds like it to me, Alan.'

I was in a no-win situation. Rosemary's touch again. If I let her go with me, I wouldn't be able to concentrate on my golf and if I refused her help, I'd offend her even more deeply than I'd already managed to do. I thought it over for a long time.

'How well do you know Greenblades?'

'I play here three times a week.'

'Thought it was men only.'

'Not since Warren took an interest.'

'Are you the first woman member?'

'The only one.'

I used to admire Australia because it seemed free from the horrors of the English class system. None of that rigid adherence to a pecking order that still holds sway, albeit in a more discreet form. I was mistaken. Australia does have a stratified society and it's based on wealth. The moneyed aristocracy call the shots and Greenblades was one of their playgrounds. It was the exclusive retreat of some of the most influential mandarins of the city who were ready to pay for the best and make sure that they got it. If Warren Oxley could buy his wife into such a club, it spoke volumes for the strength of his bank balance and for his powers of persuasion. It also revealed his love for her.

'What have you got to lose?' she challenged.

'My peace of mind.'

'I might surprise you.'

She'd been doing that ever since I met her. Diane Reinhold was no conventional woman. I could not imagine anyone else in her position getting up so early

64

for the dubious privilege of carrying my golf bag around a wind-swept course. Her motivation must have been strong. I did not want to give her a slap in the face.

After thinking it over, I nodded. Three holes. I could get rid of her then and continue the practice round on my own. She would only be a temporary nuisance.

Diane smiled her thanks and took charge of my bag. We set off towards the first tee. Greenblades was very much an unknown quantity to me. All that I'd been given when I accepted the invitation to take part in the Skins Game was a promotional brochure about the country club itself and a card of the course. The latter had aroused my interest at once.

HOLE	YARDAGE	PAR
1	204	3
2	420	4
3	271	4
4	590	5
5	397	4
6	415	4
7	173	3
8	531	5
9	384	4
10	131	3
11	600	5
12	588	5
13	315	4
14	190	3
15	445	4
16	409	4
17	267	4
18	468	4

Out	3385 yards	par 36
In	3413 yards	par 36
Total	6798 yards	par 72
Record	68	Rod Melville
		Inaugural tournament, 1987

Greenblades was no soft touch. If the mighty Rod Melville had only been able to steal four strokes off it, then it had to be a testing course. I did not relish the two par fives back to back and I suspected that the proximity of the sea would make some of the shorter par fours much more perilous than they looked on paper. What caught my eye at once, however, was the opening par three. It is rare to begin a round of golf with a short hole and Royal Lytham and St Anne's is one of the few championship courses that does this. That first hole is comparatively benign and allows you to get off to a safe start. This was not the case at Greenblades. As we stood on the tee, I saw the dangers all too clearly.

The fairway climbed steadily up to the green which was set on a raised plateau that mushroomed up out of the ground. Heavily bunkered at the front, it had undulations that always worked against you. A cruel pin placement obliged you to putt downhill and left you very little green to play with. Getting on to the narrow plateau would be difficult enough but staying on it would not be easy either. Hundreds of over-hit putts must have rolled down the gradient until they found sand.

I decided to try out my caddie.

'What's at the back of the green?'

'Fringe rough then a steep slope to oblivion.'

'So what's my best line?'

'Drop it deep on the right-hand side with plenty of backspin. It should get a good roll from the contours and bring you reasonably close to the flag. Normally, you could probably reach it with a 2-iron. Since you're hitting into the teeth of the wind, I'd suggest a 4-wood.'

'And what would you use?'

'Have to be a driver,' she said airily. 'I don't have your distance from the tee. I'd grip lower to get more control and to shorten the shot a little. Like me to show you?'

'Be my guest.'

Diane Reinhold produced a golf glove from her pocket and slipped it on to her right hand. She then removed the hood from my driver and lifted the club out. It was longer than she was used to and tailored to my needs rather than hers but she did not complain. Tee and ball appeared from her pocket as if brought along in readiness for this moment. After a few practice swings she was quietly confident. She stepped back a few yards to size up her shot then came forward again to address her ball.

Taking time to compose herself, she drew the clubhead back in an arc then let fly. Her swing was functional rather than graceful but there was no denying its effectiveness. The ball soared high and true before slowing in the wind and dropping at the rear of the green. By the time it had finished rolling backwards, it was no more than twenty yards from the hole. I was duly impressed.

'Good shot!'

'Too far left. Given myself a tricky putt.'

'I'd settle for it.'

In the event, I settled for far less. Using a 4-wood from the tee, I hit a high, wayward ball that found the right-hand edge of the green only to roll off it into a deep bunker. Diane said nothing. I appreciated that.

She knew what she was doing and did it well. I could not fault her. She only spoke when I invited a comment and her advice was both sound and concise. Her judgement of distance was uncanny. I could rely on her. By the time I sank my putt on the third green, I forgot that I meant to dispense with her services there and then. We were going the whole way together. I needed her.

Golf courses are like crossword puzzles. You have to try to get into the mind of the person who created them. Once you understand that mentality – with all its quirks and weaknesses – you find it easier to solve the puzzle. The architect behind Greenblades was a cunning fox with sadistic inclinations. He gave you stunning vistas that distracted you from the hazards he had so liberally scattered. He exposed you to wind and water in the most nerve-racking way. He rejoiced in the principle of crime and punishment. Most of his fairways threaded through copses of paperbark trees or eucalyptus. There were dozens of seductive opportunities to go out of bounds or to lose your ball.

Greenblades was one continuous ambush. Each hole had a distinctive character and forced you to think. Survival was the watchword: conquest was usually a fantasy. There was no respite, no comfortable hole where you could take a breather and gather your strength for the next big test. It was pressure golf all the way. I saw Rod Melville's course record in a new light. It was almost miraculous.

After being forced to drive across a hundred and fifty yards of open water at the fourteenth, I was glad when we swung back in towards woodland. The fifteenth hole was a long narrow corridor between high trees. An expert in the techniques of slow torture had bunkered the fairway. Any more sand and they could have built beach huts on it. The immediate temptation was to try to clear them with the driver but the shot would have to be straight. Even a modest hook or a slice would involve you in a game of hide and seek. The crosswind did not help. Just when I thought my tee shot was safe, a sudden gust caught it in the palm of its hand and threw it hard into the foliage off to the left. Deciding that the ball would probably be unplayable – if we actually found it – I hit a second tee shot. It was thirty yards shorter but it missed the bunkers and stayed on the fairway.

As we walked side by side towards it, I caught a glimpse of something flitting at speed through the trees on our left, heading in the direction where my first ball must have landed. It vanished almost as soon as it came and I dismissed it as a trick of the light. My full attention was needed to play the next shot. It was the finest I hit all morning, a crisp 3-iron that stayed low before landing just short of the green and rolling up bravely to rest within six feet of the hole.

I got my first birdie. Of sorts.

Elation changed to apprehension when I stood on the next tee. The sixteenth hole was the worst yet, a sharp dog-leg to the left with taller trees and even larger bunkers. A series of mounds ran across the fairway in parallel lines to give it the appearance of a grassy switchback ride. All these hazards paled beside the surging threat to the right. The sea was pounding the rocks below and sending up spray that reached the edge of the fairway itself. I wondered how many balls must already have met a watery grave. Vic would doubtless have the statistics at his fingertips.

My caddie waited patiently till I spoke.

'Get me out of this one, Diane.'

'There are three ways to play this hole.'

'Bad, worse and there-goes-another-Titleist!'

'No,' she said seriously. 'Safe, daring and sheer bloody madness.'

'What's the safe way?'

'Take a 4-iron and pick your spot between the bunkers at the turn. The daring route is to use a 3-wood and stay close to the trees where the fairway is much more level. The extra yardage will take you well past the angle and give you a good approach shot from the right.'

'And sheer bloody madness?'

'Take your driver and hit straight across the water to that headland. It's a carry of 220 yards but you'll be ideally placed for your second shot.'

'Anyone ever do it?'

'Rod Melville.'

'I only feel daring today.'

Given the strength of the wind and the thickness of the woodland, it was a very dangerous tee shot. Unless I held my line, I could be in among the tree trunks again. I went through my usual routine, addressed the ball then played the shot. It flirted with the foliage all the way then landed exactly where Diane had predicted. I began to wish I'd succumbed to sheer bloody madness.

We marched along the fairway in the shade of the trees. Diane was to my left, silent but totally involved in our practice round. I was gazing over to the sea on my right, weighing up the chances of emulating Rod Melville during my two visits to the hole in the Skins Game. My attention was diverted from my caddie and I forgot all about her until I heard her cry of alarm. By the time I turned to her, it was far too late.

She was being bundled into the trees by two figures in denims, T-shirts and black balaclavas. Before I could even try to help her, something large, soft and pungent was clamped over my mouth by an unseen assailant. His other arm was around my neck and I fought to shake him off my back but my resistance wilted. Red-hot needles shot up my nostrils and down my throat. My lungs were on fire, my mind was a furnace and my limbs refused to function.

I was being burned alive.

Golf was over for the day.

CHAPTER THREE

HOW LONG I WAS UNCONSCIOUS I do not know but I had the most vivid dream to keep me occupied. All my phobias ganged up on me to get in a kick while I was down. I found myself lying on a trolley in my pyjamas, being pushed at speed along a never-ending hospital corridor with glaring lights set into its ceiling. Dressed as a nurse, Rosemary walked beside me and berated me for not taking more care on a golf course. Vic, in the guise of a hospital porter, drifted in to give me facts and figures about the high mortality rate on the sixteenth hole at Greenblades. Rod Melville, a fellow victim, swathed in bandages from head to foot and passing me on another trolley, groaned in agreement. I was to blame. I should have driven more carefully from the tee.

Whenever I tried to sit up and speak, Rosemary subdued me by putting a compress firmly across my mouth and nose. The red hot needles did their stuff again and I sank back helplessly. We then banged our way through a series of double doors until we came to the operating theatre. I was wheeled under a huge battery of lights and examined by unseen hands. Faces flashed into my vision.

A leering Clive Phelps asked me how I'd made out with my caddie. Harvey Jansen, with six children in his arms, told me to stay awake during my operation so that I could describe it in detail in my book. Jan Cummings asked if I had any complaints about my accommodation. When I started to make them, a peremptory Warren Oxley told me to shut up. Herm Wexler's anxious visage came into view – 'See, Al? I told you that course was a gorilla.' Mary Anne soothed him and ignored me.

Then all of them spun round and round together until they coalesced into the face I least wanted to see. It was my father. His gaze had dark satisfaction. There was that usual, sneering, contemptuous I-told-you-so look which had haunted me for so many years. He was in uniform. I was now in a police cell. My wrists were handcuffed to the trolley. Everything I'd spent a lifetime escaping now crowded in upon me. His voice deafened my ears. His boots marked time on my chest. His bitterness consumed me. He ticketed my golf clubs for the trial so that they could be used against me as exhibits by the prosecution.

His face hurled towards mine like an angry punch. I closed my eyes and tensed against a blow that never came. When I dared to look up again, I was back in the operating theatre and Rosemary was leaning over me, but only for a second because her features changed imperceptibly into those of Diane Reinhold. Reproof became concern. Coldness was replaced with warmth. I had a friend at last. Diane leaned forward to seal that friendship with a tender kiss but her tongue suddenly lengthened by several inches and she slobbered all over me. With my last ounce of energy, I swung an arm to brush her away.

Rosemary applied the compress once more and I became inert. The battery of lights intensified their glare. People gathered around the trolley then the surgeon bent over his patient. It was David Ridger. He was going to perform the operation with the car key of a new Jaguar. As he bathed my forehead with a swab of cotton wool, he insisted that he would pay the bill for the medication.

David pointed the tip of his key and the laser beam of his questions cut straight through my skull. I cried out in pain and Lynette came running to help me but she could not get in through the locked doors.

David had the key.

When I yelled again, the hospital disappeared and I was back at Greenblades once more, being pushed along on the trolley at top speed over very uneven terrain. I fought hard to clear my head and made a supreme effort to sit up.

'Take it easy, Mr Saxon.'

'Where am I?'

'Safe and sound.'

'Mm.'

'Just lie back down.'

'Who are you?'

'A doctor. You'll be all right.'

The haze cleared and I saw that I was lying on the massage table in the locker room. A middle-aged man in a fawn suit was bending solicitously over me. Vic lurked nearby with a shifty expression. He was torn between anxiety over me and fear for himself.

I put a hand to my forehead but there was no blood. The operation had been a bad dream organised on my behalf by friends and acquaintances. I was relieved.

'You were lucky,' said the doctor.

'That's nice to know.'

'They hit you with chloroform.'

'I went out like a light.'

'That's the idea,' he explained. 'Chloroform was the favourite form of anaesthetic in the old days. It completely superseded ether because it's about three times as potent and much more suitable for longer operations. Main drawback is that it's very easy to exceed the dose. Chloroform can kill as well as cure.'

'That's comforting!'

'There's worse, Mr Saxon. It quickly decomposes in air, especially in the presence of sunlight. Carbonyl chloride and hydrochloric acid are produced. The former is highly dangerous when chloroform is used as an anaesthetic. That's why they used to store the liquid in the dark.' He helped me up into a sitting position. 'It's a sunny day out there. You were lucky.'

'What about Diane?'

The doctor exchanged a look with Vic then put a few items into his bag before snapping it shut. A car was heard approaching rapidly over the gravel then skidding to a halt at the rear of the building. It was not long before Warren Oxley came surging in through the door with another man at his heels.

Oxley glanced at me, shot a look at Vic then took the doctor aside. They had a muttered conversation together. The other man who had come in was Lee Whitfield, one of the business associates I'd met at Point Piper on the previous evening. He was a thin, angular man of middle height with brown hair slicked straight back and divided by a centre parting that was as livid as an operation scar. I wondered if his barber had used chloroform.

Whitfield was quiet, impassive and watchful. Like most of the people around Oxley, he was in his early thirties. The doctor ended his report and was given a valedictory pat on the shoulder. He went quickly out and Whitfield closed the door after him, standing in front of it to make sure that we were not interrupted. Oxley stared at Vic again and tapped his foot slowly on the floor. The chauffeur was scared and apologetic.

Warren Oxley came across to me. His manner was crisp as if we were discussing a slight hitch in an important business deal. His fury was carefully reined in.

'How d'you feel, Alan?'

'I think I'll live.'

'What happened?'

'You tell me.'

'How many were there?'

'Three.'

'Where did they jump you?'

'On the sixteenth,' I said ruefully. 'I was in prime position to play a 5-iron into the green.'

'Let's go over it very carefully.'

'I don't remember all that much.'

'Try. It's vital.'

'Do my best, Warren.'

I recounted my story in broad outline, keeping back a few details for my own use. Since the doctor had told me about the chloroform, I was very keen to meet the man who administered it so I did not mention that he must have been exceptionally tall and powerful if he could restrain me from behind while applying the pad. Oxley, Whitfield and Vic listened intently. They showed me only a brusque sympathy. I concluded my tale with a shrug.

'That's about it, I'm afraid.'

'It'll do for starters,' said Oxley.

'Mind telling me how I got here?'

'I brought you,' said Vic. 'In a golf buggy.'

That accounted for the rough ride over grass in my dream. The tearaway trolley had been chauffeured by Vic.

'When did you find me?' I asked.

'Soon after.'

'Not soon enough!' noted Oxley.

'They went out of sight,' said Vic lamely.

'You let them get out of sight.'

Oxley nodded to Whitfield who opened the door and took Vic outside. The chauffeur was clearly in disgrace. I felt sufficiently recovered to put my feet on the ground. My legs were weak but they supported me. Oxley stepped in close.

'Now tell me what really happened.'

'I've already done so.'

'You're holding something back.'

'Why should I do that?'

'Bloody-mindedness.'

'There's nothing else, Warren.'

'Don't play around with me.'

'You know the lot.'

'You're lying,' he said.

'I've told you the truth.'

'Fill in the bits you missed out.'

All that Warren Oxley did was to stand there calmly and look at me but I felt completely intimidated. He had something in store for me that was far worse than a dose of chloroform. To keep him at bay, I strutted around the room and worked myself up into a mock rage.

'Get off my back, will you! Christ Almighty! I came here today to play a practice round and what happens? I'm lumbered with a caddie I don't want and then pounced on by some maniac out on the course. Honestly, Warren, it was all over in seconds. I heard the scream, turned to see the two of them hustling her away then had this thing clapped over my mouth like a gas mask. That was it. When you take a sniff of chloroform, you don't then stand round to take names, addresses and detailed descriptions of all present. I was a goner. Miracle is that I can recall any bloody thing!' I stormed back to him. 'So leave me alone, okay? I'm a golfer not a private detective. I can't give you an exhaustive report. What I know is what you heard. For God's sake – I was one of the *victims*!'

He scrutinized me then gave an apologetic nod.

'Sorry, Alan.'

'What sort of a golf club is this?'

'You had cover.'

'Vic?'

'He was supposed to tail you all the way.'

I realised why the chauffeur had brought binoculars. He had kept us under surveillance from a discreet distance. I remembered the car which had followed us that morning.

'Why did I need a bodyguard?'

'You didn't, Alan. She did.'

'Diane?'

'She's been kidnapped.'

Concern for myself had largely blotted out fears for the safety of my caddie. When last seen, Diane was being bundled off through the undergrowth. Vic had been on hand to prevent just such a mishap. He'd failed in his duty.

'Why did they snatch her?' I said.

'That's our business.'

'Was she under threat?'

'Not really.'

'Then why assign Vic to ride shotgun?'

'Just forget it, will you?'

'Warren, this is your wife we're talking about. How can you be so relaxed about it? Someone's jumped on me and kidnapped her. Aren't you going to call the police?'

'We'll handle this our way.'

'But she could be in great danger.'

'She is,' he said. 'Calling in the cops will only make it worse. That was their first condition. No cops.'

'They?'

'I had a phone call.'

Warren Oxley crossed to look out of the window and

77

straightened his tie. There was still no sign of real emotion in the wake of what had happened. Diane had been taken by force and he was treating it as a business negotiation which had gone awry. He motioned me across and we looked out towards the first tee.

'What do you think of Greenblades?'

'Too many baddies on the sixteenth.'

'I asked you a serious question.'

'It's a good course, Warren. A true test of golf.'

'So we made the right choice for the Skins Game?'

'Diane wouldn't think so.'

'Forget Diane,' he snapped, rounding on me. 'You're out of this now. Completely. As far as you're concerned, nothing untoward happened out there today. Programme the whole thing out of your mind.'

'But I can't do that.'

'You'll have to do it, mate. Or you'll wish you'd stayed back home in that fucking motor caravan of yours. Alan Saxon came to Australia to play golf. That's what he's going to do. Carry on as if everything was perfectly normal. Understand?'

'Tall order, Warren.'

'You can handle it.'

'How do you know?'

'Because you don't want to fly home in a box.'

Vic was silent and morose on the journey back to my hotel. I couldn't coax a single word out of him, still less a smile. The chauffeur had made a blunder and he would have to suffer the consequences. Judging by the sombre expression on his face, he was trying to assess what those consequences would be as we edged our way through the noonday traffic. We were not followed.

When we reached the Hilton, I had to open my own door to get out of the car. In the heat of the kidnap, my golf bag had been pulled off Diane and thrown to the ground. Vic retrieved it when he found me. He now lifted the bag out of the boot and carried it into the foyer. His mind was whirring busily away and he snapped his fingers.

'Beverly!' he said to himself. 'That bitch!'

'Who?'

He looked blank then shook his head dismissively.

'Nothing.'

'Thanks for the lift.'

'Need me again?'

'Possibly.'

'Here's the number.' He fished a card out from inside his uniform and handed it to me. 'Ring any time. I won't be far away.'

'Right.'

Vic took his leave and I went straight up to my room. I was still light-headed after my close encounter at Greenblades and a restorative whirlpool bath was high on my list of priorities. Something else, however, came first. I rang Clive.

'Clive?'

'Saxon! Where are you, old son? Been trying to contact you all morning.'

'I was playing a round of golf.'

'Why didn't you tell me?'

'I was on the tee at eight o'clock.'

'Ye gods! Didn't open my peepers till nine.'

'That means you slept alone last night.'

'Intermittently.'

I'd tracked Clive down in the bar at his hotel. He sounded as if he was on his third drink. It also meant that he was writing something. Clive Phelps did all his best work in an alcoholic haze.

'Can I try something out on you?' he said.

'No.'

'I will, anyway.'

'Then make it quick.'

'As the art mistress said to the gardener.'

'And spare me the sexual banter.'

'Spoilsport! Okay, grab this. "Golf is neither a recreation nor a tiresome duty, but a serious passion demanding and receiving all one's powers of intelligence, concentration, ardour and sensitivity". Classy, eh?'

'Who said it?'

'I just did, you numbskull!'

'Originally, I meant. Sounds like a quotation.'

'It is. Berlioz.'

'The composer?'

'Yep. Old Hector himself.'

'Berlioz never played golf.'

'That's why he said it about music instead. I'm just adapting his words of wisdom to my chosen subject. Title of the article is "Serious Passion". I'm writing my own Symphonie Fantastique about the game.' I heard him finish his drink and order another. 'How was Greenblades?'

'Murderous.'

'So I've heard. Any chance of a round together?'

'Maybe later. You've got work to do first.'

'Have I?'

'Find out all you can about Diane Reinhold.'

'Oxley's wife?' He laughed warningly. 'Keep well clear of her, Alan. If you wish to remain whole, that is. Warren the Ox is the jealous type. You practise your swing with her and he'll cut off your balls and send them back to you in a jar of pickled onions.'

'It's nothing like that, Clive.'

'Then what is it?'

'Diane was responsible for this Skins Game. I want to know why and how. Oh, and while you're at it, dig up all you can about Oxley himself.'

'Are you joking? That'd take me years.'

'See what you can do in an afternoon.'

'I've got high hopes of the receptionist here.'

'This is important, Clive. Please.'

'What's in it for me?'

'The glow of satisfaction that comes from helping an old friend in his hour of need.'

'Bollocks!'

'I knew I could rely on you.'

'What about Greenblades?'

'Pick you up at five.'

'Perfect! She goes back on duty at four-thirty.'

'One more thing …'

'I've got enough on my plate already.'

'Does the name Beverly mean anything to you?'

'Beverly? Beverly?' He flipped through the pages of his mental diary and chuckled. 'Of course. The Jersey Open last year. She was the Liaison Officer or something. Certainly liaised pretty good with me.'

'Not that Beverly,' I said.

'Which one, then?' He displayed the range like a car salesman. 'Beverly up at Troon earlier this year? Bouncy Bev at Sunningdale? That randy press officer in Chicago who liked to keep her hand in while her husband was on night shifts? And what about that tour guide over in Madrid? Wasn't she called Beverly?'

'This one is Australian.'

'What's her second name?'

'That's what I want you to tell me.'

'But there must be a bevy of Beverlies here.'

'This one's special.'

'In what way?'

'She has some connection with Oxley.'

'Oh, that Beverly! Why didn't you say?'

'You know her?'

'Of course. Beverly Nashe.'

'Never heard of her.'

'Don't you ever read the papers?'

'I'm too busy studying the Gideon Bible.'

'Beverly Nashe. The famous Beverly Nashe.'

'So who is she?'

'Oxley's first wife.'

It was a small private hospital on the outskirts of Sydney. Set in its own grounds, it was a solid and unexciting Edwardian building which had recently been renovated. A taxi had taken me there in just under half an hour. I'd dispensed with Vic's services on this occasion because he would have reported my visit to his employer. Since the disappearance of Diane Reinhold, my chauffeur had also become my shadow. I preferred him as the former – statistics notwithstanding. A promising friendship between us had been blighted for good.

I went in through the main door of the hospital with some trepidation. My dream had symbolic content and I still caught a faint whiff of the anaesthetic. A bright-eyed receptionist fielded my enquiry and gave me lucid instructions. I was soon padding along a corridor before turning into a side ward. Off it were four private rooms and he was in the first.

'Alan! Great to see you, mate!'

'How are you, Rod?'

'I've had better times in bed.'

'You don't look too bad.'

'Not since they put all the pieces back together.'

Rod Melville was one of those grotesquely healthy men who might just have come off duty as a lifeguard at Bondi Beach. Even when he was stretched out in bed with an arm in plaster and copious bandaging, he was a picture of fitness. His big, bronzed face was split with a grin and he reached out to shake my hand.

'Appreciate this, mate.'

'I wanted to see how you were getting on.'

'Take a seat.'

'Thanks.'

I moved the armchair closer to the bed and lowered myself into it. Rod Melville was obviously in the right place. The medical facilities were superb and he had radio, television, a video recorder and a compact disc player at his disposal. Table, walls and windowsills were festooned with Get Well cards. He was more than just a patient. Rod was a celebrity. For the pretty nurses who kept flitting in and out of his room, the novelty of his presence had not yet worn off.

'Sorry to hear the news,' I said.

'Bloody maddening! I was all set to scoop the pool at Greenblades then this happens. Still, my loss is your gain, mate. You'll be able to grab the money in handfuls.'

'Herm Wexler might put a stop to that. So might Sam Limsong if he's at his peak.'

'They don't have your know-how.'

'There's always Gil Jericho.'

'Don't mention that bastard!' he growled. 'I got a sneaky feeling that he helped to put me in here so he could take my place. Gil's always been jealous of my Aston Martin.'

'Is that what you were driving?'

'Yes. Cruising along near Broken Bay. We've got a little place just north of there. You must come up and stay with us some time.'

'I'd like that.'

Rod Melville was being unduly modest. His little place was a huge, sprawling, modern bungalow with ample garaging for his collection of cars. There was a nine-hole golf course in the garden and a private lake

83

on which he could sail with his wife and children. The game which was our life had given him all the trappings of success: I had to settle for a motor caravan and some bitter-sweet memories.

He adjusted his position, then continued his story.

'Anyway, there I am, driving along with not a soul in sight. I couldn't have been doing more than seventy or eighty. Then this Porsche comes out of a side-road up ahead of me and cuts right across my path. I thought there was room to mount the verge and go past him on the inside but he carved me up and forced me into the bushes. Before I could control the car, we went slap bang into an outcrop of rock.'

'Much damage?'

'A complete wreck!' he said in aggrieved tones. 'It was custom-built, that motor. The pride of my fleet. How can I replace it?' He surveyed his own injuries. 'I took a battering but it was the Aston Martin that came off worst. I mean, I'll be out of here at the end of the week and back in business before you can shout "Fore!" Not that lovely old motor. Smashed to pieces. It's criminal!'

'So it wasn't an accident, Rod?'

'No way, mate.'

'What do the police say?'

'They're still working on the case. They found the Porsche the following day, abandoned in Ku-ring-gai Chase National Park.'

'Stolen?'

'From some bloke down in Woollongong.'

'The whole thing sounds premeditated.'

'Can't understand it, Alan,' he said in the voice of someone who had always enjoyed universal popularity in his home country. 'Christ – I'm Rod Melville! Who could do something like that to *me*?'

'I hope we find out.'

We speculated on the matter for some time then I got him talking about Greenblades. He boasted frankly about his course record but gave me valuable advice when telling me how he had achieved it. Rod Melville had his vices – bragging about his virtues, for instance – but I always got on well with him. Everything was up front. He never tried to deceive or manipulate. There was a basic honesty about the man that shone through at all times. It was the reason I liked him and hated Gil Jericho. While the former said everything to your face, the latter made you fear for your back.

Rod used a hand to comb his thick black hair.

'Have you met Warren yet?' he said.

'Last night.'

'What do you think of him?'

'A bit too epic for me.'

He laughed. 'Warren's okay. Good bloke. One of us.'

'Us?'

'Lives on his wits and rides his luck. Isn't that what we do, mate? He does the same thing a different way.'

'A very different way.'

'Where'd you meet him?'

'A welcoming party at Point Piper.'

'Was the new wife there?'

'Yes. Diane was playing the gracious hostess.'

'What's she like?'

'Haven't you met her?'

'No,' he said. 'Living in the States nine months a year has its drawbacks. You lose touch. They got married while I was in Florida. I remember something in the paper about it but that was all. So who is this Diane Reinhold? What's she got that can hook a guy like Warren Oxley? I mean, let's face it, he can have almost any woman he likes. Why did he choose her?'

'She's … out of the ordinary.'

'Attractive?'

'Very.'

'Sexy?'

'In a restrained sort of way.'

'How did Warren seem with her?'

'Undemonstrative but quietly happy.'

'Well, that makes a bloody change! You should've seen him and Beverly together. They went right over the top. Kept shoving the Big Romance right in your face like a custard pie. Kissing, cuddling – they were always at it. Someone called them Sydney's Ideal Couple but all that groping in public used to make me puke.'

'Diane is not into that kind of thing.'

'Then she's one up on the first wife.'

'Who is Beverly Nashe?'

'You really don't know?'

'Britain is a long, long way away, Rod.'

'Suppose so,' he agreed. 'It's just that Beverly is such a star down here. She started off as a journo. Worked on this women's magazine. You should see her, mate. A real, hot-shot glamour girl – with brains to match. When she was still only twenty-five, she became editor. The mag really took off then. So did Beverly. Campaigning journalism. That meant stirring up the shit to increase circulation.'

'How did she meet her husband?'

'On television. She had her own chat show by then. Batting the breeze with anyone in the news. She had me on there once. Gave me such a roasting that I had to slap her down.' He grinned broadly. 'I don't take that crap from a sheila, even if she is good-looking enough to give the Pope a hard-on for a week.'

'Did Warren go on her show?'

'Yes, Alan. He was just starting to make it big as a corporate raider. Firing at anything that moved with a takeover bid. Beverly gave him a tough time. Didn't he think that his methods were too brutal? Was it true that all venture capitalists were monsters? And so on. Warren took it on the chin. After the show, he asked her out.'

'Did she accept?'

'Not on your life, mate!'

'Then how did they get together?'

'Took him best part of a bloody year.' He chuckled as he recalled it. 'First of all, he buys her magazine so that he employs her. Beverly resigns and goes to another one. He buys that as well. She concentrates on her telly work so he puts in a bid for the station. Warren Oxley is just too powerful by now. There's nowhere in Australia she can hide from him. So she gave in and agreed to have lunch with him.'

'What happened?'

'They married a week later. Spent their honeymoon cruising around the South Sea Islands on his yacht. It was renamed *The Beverly.*'

'It must have been some lunch!'

'I bet the waiter got the tip of a lifetime.'

'How long were they married?'

'Six years.'

'Happily?'

'In public. Too happily.'

'And in private?'

'Who can say?'

'Why did they get divorced?'

'Dunno, mate, but it wasn't Beverly's idea, that's for certain. She's a bit of a one for what you might call the spectacular gesture.'

'She created a scene?'

'Worse. Remember that yacht he named after her? When she heard that he was going to spend his second honeymoon on it, she set fire to the thing. Burned to a cinder.'

'Wasn't she arrested?'

'Warren refused to bring a prosecution. He explained it away as an unfortunate accident and the police were happy to treat it as a domestic squabble that didn't concern them. Oh, Beverly is quite a woman!'

'Yet Diane Reinhold replaced her.'

'That's the big mystery, Alan. How?'

As I was driven away from the hospital, I had plenty of food for thought. Rod Melville had answered some questions but created several more. When I first met Warren Oxley, my gut reaction was to loathe him and all that he represented. I now came to see that we might be indissolubly linked. Both of us were at the mercy of a vengeful ex-wife. The fate of Diane Reinhold had drawn us together. The search for her kidnapper – like my own grim search – might lie in the dynamics of a failed marriage.

That was the best place to start.

Clive Phelps turned up trumps. When I met him in the foyer of his hotel, he handed me a large brown envelope that contained all I needed. He'd got a friend at the *Sydney Morning Herald* to raid the cuttings library and photostat selected items. I had the steamy story of Warren Oxley and his two wives under plain cover.

'Thanks, Clive. I'm really grateful.'

'I'll give you ample opportunity to prove it.'

'Don't mention this in front of Vic.'

'Who?'

'The chauffeur.'

'How can I mention it in front of him when we'll be sitting behind him? Anyway, what's the big secret?'

'Tell you later.'

We went out to the Mercedes, put his golf bag into the boot alongside my own, then set off. For all his sterling qualities, Clive is not the most discreet of men and there was always the chance that he might say something to alert Vic. I decided to silence my friend completely. There was one sure way.

'Hey, Vic …'

'Yeah?'

'Clive was asking about the Harbour Bridge.'

'Was he?'

'When was it opened?'

'In 1932.' Vic was away. 'Before that, most people crossed the harbour by ferries. In 1927 there were some forty-seven million ferry passengers. That same year, the Watsons' Bay ferry *Greycliffe* and the liner *Tahiti* collided. Thirty-seven people were killed.'

Clive semaphored wildly at me. He could not remember asking for anything like this. Vic hit his stride.

'The Bridge was built during the Depression and nicknamed the Iron Lung. It's the largest – though not the longest – steel arch bridge in the world. The span is 503 metres. Fourteen hundred workmen were employed in its construction. It was opened on March 19th, 1932. It has a roadway, two footways and four railway lines.'

'Tell Clive about the rivets.'

Vic did just that. We were soon in Greenblades.

In the locker room, Clive turned on me.

'What was all that garbage in aid of?' he demanded.

'I thought you'd be fascinated.'

'Balls! That man has as much fascination as a Speak-Your-Weight machine. And a lot less use! Why the hell did you unleash him on me like that?'

'It helped to pass the time.'

'So did the Chinese torture – and it's an even bet which was worse!' Clive dumped his bag down and tapped me on the chest with his finger. 'What's going on, Saxon?'

'We're about to play a round of golf.'

'Don't give me that. Something is up.'

'Is it?'

'I have a sixth sense.'

'Clive Phelps. Golf writer and clairvoyant!'

'Stop taking the piss. What is happening?'

'Tell you later.'

'Now!' he insisted.

'Later, Clive.'

'Right this minute.'

'Trust me.'

'As the bishop said to the actress.'

'Let's play golf.'

Greenblades was fairly busy. Members had arrived in numbers to play a round after a day's work or to trade stories in the clubhouse. I got several waves of welcome and some cheerful barracking. Gil Jericho was now the local hero. I was an upstart Pom who would soon be put in his place. The banter took us to the first tee.

We dispensed with caddies and borrowed golf carts because I didn't want anyone else with us. Clive chose a motorised cart but I preferred to pull mine. The wind had dropped but the course would still be a stern test. As I looked down the fairway, I remembered the exquisite shot that Diane had played with my driver. I'd scorned her offer to caddie for me yet finished up respecting her golfing knowledge. It was one of the reasons that made me want to do all I could to find her. If she had not put herself out to take me around Greenblades, she might not have been kidnapped. I was partly to blame.

Clive was eyeing the green with some alarm.

'Nasty, brutish and short.'

'Think of England.'

'Are all the holes as tough as this?'

'No. This is the easy one.'

'I knew I should've worn my brown trousers!'

He continued to moan but I could see that he was keen to tackle Greenblades. It was an irresistible challenge to a true golfer and Clive Phelps was most certainly that. As well as writing superbly about the game, he could play it like a dream. With less drink, less weight and more practice, he could have made a living in the professional ranks but that would have been to deny his essential character. Wine, women and a few thousand words a week on golf was his idea of earthly paradise.

Clive had found it. I was still looking for mine.

I hit the green with a 3-iron and he did the same with a 4-wood. The undulations tormented us but we both managed par. It was an encouraging start. Somehow the next hole did not look quite so daunting now.

We were playing a different type of game. Clive was fighting to get the measure of the course while I was more concerned to explore its perils. I hit tee shots into the heavy rough, I found the deepest bunkers, I chose the worst possible lies. I wanted to test out all the hazards and learn to recover from them. The chances were that I'd encounter some of them during the Skins Game itself. Familiarity breeds confidence.

Clive was having an erratic round. After relative success over the first few holes, he hit a bad patch, found his touch again at the turn then came to grief at the consecutive par fives. The short fourteenth rewarded his boldness with a par whereas I sliced my tee shot into the rolling waves below. Greenblades gave us a thorough examination. We were stretched by its difficulties but exhilarated by the fight. Both of us were completely absorbed in our golf.

Then we walked across to the fifteenth tee. Clive had the honour and sent a screaming drive down the long, tree-lined avenue. I addressed my own ball but I was unable to hit the shot I planned. An inner voice seemed to issue a command and I found myself hooking badly. It was not without purpose. As my ball searched the sky then plunged down into the trees off to the left, I saw something flash through the undergrowth as I'd done on my previous visit. I also felt a long wet tongue licking me as I lay on a hospital trolley.

Dropping my club, I sprinted down the fairway.

'Where are you going?' yelled Clive.

'To see a man about a dog.'

I went into the trees about fifty yards short of my ball and dodged my way between the trunks. There was no sign of anybody – human or animal – but my instinct drove me on. Panting for breath, I came to a halt beside a plane tree and listened carefully. The rustling sound came from up ahead. I let my ears guide me forward until I saw evidence of movement among the bushes. There was no point in trying to chase him. Four canine legs would always outrun mine. I had to try friendship.

'Here, boy! Come on! Over here!'

The bushes stopped moving. I was being watched.

'Come on! This way! Say hello!'

The dog was weighing me up from its hiding place. I whistled softly and went down on one knee to beckon the animal to me. Eventually, it worked. The dog emerged with caution from a clump of bushes some thirty yards away and took a few circumspect steps in my direction. I repeated the whistle and patted my thigh.

'Come on! I won't hurt you.'

It was a golden-haired Labrador with large eyes and a beautiful coat. When I saw it was a bitch, I realised why my call of 'boy' had not coaxed her out. Advancing

92

towards me with a mixture of hesitation and curiosity, she got within five yards and stopped. I waddled my way carefully towards her and got within touching range. She looked as if she would bolt at a moment's notice so I took some time to make soothing noises. Her tongue came out and she panted contentedly. I reached forward to pat her gently on the head. She gave me a wag of her tail but the suspicion did not vanish entirely from those eyes.

The animal was well-fed and well-groomed. Its owner would surely attach a name tag to the collar. I stroked her neck, felt for the collar amid her golden hair and located a copper disc. Her name was engraved on it above her address. I memorised both immediately and I was only just in time.

'Saxon! Where the fuck are you!'

Clive was coming to find me. The dog didn't like the sound of his voice or the way that he was rampaging through the undergrowth. She turned tail and darted back to the bushes in which she'd been hiding. Having picked something up in her jaws, she tore off through the trees as if she had somewhere important to go. I was sorry to lose her but she'd told me what I wanted to know.

Man's best friend might be able to help a lady.

'Saxon!'

'Over here, Clive!'

'How long does it take you to have a slash?'

'That isn't why I came.'

'Then why?'

He lurched out at me as I used a pencil to write something on my scorecard. Clive looked over my shoulder at the name I'd put next to the number fifteen.

'Sheba?'

'Yes.'

'What kind of a score is that?'

93

'Might even be a hole-in-one.'

Clubhouses are the same the world over. It is nothing to do with their design or with the amount of money that has been invested in them. Whether it's Reigate or Rangoon, New York or New Delhi, the same basic types always seem to congregate, activated by much the same issues. Greenblades was no different. It had its uncritical admirer who wants to buy you a drink, its lifelong duffer who's convinced that you hold the key to his improvement, its smug denigrator who tries to put you in your place over the foolish way you tackled his home course, the compulsive name-dropper who claims to be an intimate of just about every pro swinging a club, the Wise Owl who thinks he has spotted the glaring weakness in your game that has held you back all these years, and the self-appointed comedian who tells you the oldest golf joke in the book as if he has just invented it. And, of course, the club bores, those loyal members of a worldwide community who possess no mirrors to show them what they are and who continue to be it with unflagging vigour.

The main topic of the evening was one I've heard debated in a hundred clubhouses – Are Woods Things Of The Past? Opinion seemed to be evenly divided between the traditionalists and the heavy metal boys. Clive and I were forced to chip in our views when we went in for a drink and the argument became more heated. Greenblades was doing what it did every night of the week and I was relieved. It was obvious that nobody knew about the kidnap of Diane Reinhold. The whole incident had been kept under wraps. It was business as usual.

Three whiskies pacified Clive slightly and almost reconciled him to the fact that he had a disastrous time at the eighteenth. The final hole was the killer punch, the one that really finished you off if you actually managed to get that far with a respectable score. At 468 yards, it was within a whisker of being a par five. Laid out like an elongated Z-bend, it frustrated the long-hitter with every punitive device at the disposal of the architect.

After eight shots, Clive tore up his scoreboard.

'What d'you think of Greenblades?' I said.

'It's not a golf course – it's a suicide pact.'

'I'm slowly learning to love it.'

'That's masochism!'

'What else is golf?'

'Fair comment.' He sighed operatically. 'Now I see why Herm Wexler is back on the tranquillisers.'

'He married his tranquilliser.'

'The lovely Mary Anne? She's gorgeous, isn't she? You've got to admire Herm's devotion to duty. Who'd want to slave over a hot golf course when you could stay at home and play hunt the thimble with her?'

I finished my own drink, shook off a couple of well-wishers and ushered Clive out. In the empty locker room, I swore him to secrecy and told him the bare facts of the kidnap. His eyes widened like something out of a Disney cartoon. Here was high drama right on the doorstep and he was the only journalist in Sydney who knew about it. I told him about the warning that Warren Oxley had issued to me. He grabbed my arm.

'Take care, Alan. Oxley is one mean hombre.'

'I noticed.'

'Keep well clear.'

'Too late. I'm involved.'

'Back off.'

'She needs my help.'

'Why do you always ignore my advice?'

'Because you're usually wrong.'

'Was I wrong about Rosemary?'

He did not realise quite how much his snap rejoinder hurt me. Clive was not one of Rosemary's fans. He strongly urged me not to marry her and told me exactly what would happen. His prophecy came true but I did not thank him for it, nor did I lay it to my heart. Confronted with the same choice again, I'd make the identical mistake.

Rosemary had that effect on me.

I put Clive into the Mercedes with his golf bag and told Vic to drive him back to the hotel while I stayed on at the club for a while.

'Want me to come back?' asked Vic.

'No thanks. I'll get a taxi.'

'Mr Oxley said to keep an eye on you.'

'Try closing it. You look tired.'

'Ring if you need me.'

'You drive off,' I said. 'Clive is all agog to hear more about the history of your wonderful city.'

Clive severed our friendship with a look.

As soon as they'd gone, I went striding off down the gravel drive. The club steward had been very helpful. When I mentioned the address to him, he knew just where it was. As I suspected, the house was within comfortable walking distance of Greenblades. Ten minutes got me there in the gathering darkness.

It was one of a clutch of dingy bungalows that were set out in a horseshoe pattern. They reminded me of the rash of prefabs that appeared in Britain after the war, temporary accommodation that has already been the permanent home of two generations. Sydney looks like a vibrant, thrusting, up-to-date city with an almost American quota of skyscraping self-confidence, but some of its suburbs are curiously shabby and old-fashioned.

The bungalow was in the middle of the horseshoe. Light from the street lamp enabled me to see that attempts had been made to jazz the property up. The tiles were new and the place had been recently painted. The curtains in the window had a lively pattern on them. At the top of the little drive, I got confirmation that this was the right house. A large kennel stood at the rear. Two golden paws protruded. Sheba was at home.

I rang the bell and heavy footsteps came plodding towards the door. When it opened, I had my warmest smile ready. He was a big, slovenly man in his sixties with a mere skim of white hair atop a pleasantly craggy face.

He recognised me at once and was astonished to see me.

'Please can I have my ball back?' I said.

A slow smile spread across his weathered face.

'Come on in, mate.'

The living room was small and rather neglected and I got the impression that he was not used to living alone. A wedding photograph stood on the mantelpiece. Beside it was one of a grey-haired woman in a flowered dress.

'Wife died three years ago,' he explained.

'Oh. I'm sorry.'

'That's when I moved out here.'

'I didn't get your name.'

'Terry. Terry Kelso.'

'Pleased to meet you.'

'Pleasure's all mine.' He laughed and slapped his thigh hard. 'Alan Saxon! Right here in my own flaming house. Amazing! If I'd told my neighbours that you'd be dropping in tonight, they'd have thought I had kangaroos in my top paddock.'

'That's why I kept it a surprise.'

'How did you know where to find me?'

I told him about my meeting with Sheba and that

97

made him open the door to let the dog in. She wagged her tail in excitement and seemed pleased to see me again. As soon as he gave the command, she lay down obediently on the rug.

'You've got her well-trained, Mr Kelso.'

'Call me Terry.'

'Did you teach her to pick up golf balls?'

'Of course.'

'Why?'

'For my collection.' He winked at Sheba who wrinkled her nose by way of a reply. 'Shall we show him? Yes, why not? Eh?' The laws of hospitality nudged him. 'Oh. I'm sorry, mate, can I get you a beer or something?'

'No thanks, Terry.'

'Tea? Coffee?'

'What's this collection you mentioned?'

'See for yourself.'

He took me along the corridor to the main bedroom of the house, opened the door with a flourish and switched on the light. I was astounded. Two whole walls were covered from floor to ceiling in golf balls. They were held in place by Polyfilla and arranged in patterns according to their colour. The yellow ones formed a series of stars against a background of white. I'd never seen so many golf balls outside a driving range. There were a couple of thousand at least.

Pride showed in Terry's face and voice.

'What d'you say to that, then?'

'Incredible!'

'Taken us three years to collect 'em all.'

'From Greenblades?'

'That's right.' He became defensive. 'It's not stealing. I mean, we only take balls that are lost in the trees. Nobody could play them out of there, anyway. It's like a jungle. We just tidy things up.' He waved an expansive arm. 'See? Any brand you care to name. Maxfli. Dunlop. Wilson. Karsten Ping Eye. Titleist. Slazenger. Spalding. Pinnacle. Ram Laser. Hogan. The lot.'

'You must really love the game.'

'I do, Alan.'

'Play it yourself?'

'No, I'm hopeless. No sense of timing. Besides, I can't really afford it. Especially at a place like Greenblades. Membership fees there are bigger than my mortgage. Rich man's game. I just like to watch.' He surveyed his collection with a smile. 'And pick up the odd souvenir from time to time.'

'How did you first get interested?'

'From trade mags,' he said happily. 'Used to have a newsagent's shop in Darlo – that's Darlinghurst. Had a free read of anything that came in. Got really turned on by golf. I couldn't wait for the mags to come in. You were on the front cover of *Australian Golf* once. Just won the Masters down in Huntingdale.'

'I remember, Terry.'

'You beat Jeff Piker in a play-off.'

'I had to beat the galleries as well that day.'

'Yeah, we Aussies do get a bit carried away.'

'Partisan is too pale a word to describe it.' I nodded at the golf balls. 'So when did you take up this little hobby?'

'When I moved up here from Darlo. Heard they were building the place and got as close as I could to it. Me and Sheba soon found a way in. Leads to that wood down the left of the fifteenth hole.'

'And you just stay there and watch?'

'Yeah, mate. We got our own grandstand seat for any tournament and you've no idea how many balls get hooked in there. Sheba's picked up thirty or more in a day.'

'What about this morning?'

'It's right over there,' he said, crossing to the bedside table to pick up a ball. 'Couldn't miss the chance of getting an Alan Saxon. Didn't know you played Titleist 384 Tour. I like the way you personalise them.' He looked defensive again. 'You don't really want it back, do you? I'll swap it for two others.'

'Keep the ball, Terry. My compliments.'

'Great. I'll put it with my Rod Melville.'

'Were you there yourself this morning?'

'Yeah. I took a picture of you on the fifteenth tee. And another of you walking down the fairway. That's my other hobby. Photography.' He patted me on the back. 'Hey, you played a beaut on to the green. I saw you sink that putt.'

'What else did you see, Terry?'

'Eh?'

'That wood sweeps around to the sixteenth hole. Did you trail us there as well?'

'No.' His shifty expression gave him away.

'I think you did.'

'Not me, mate. Too old. Move slowly.'

'Sheba certainly followed us.'

'She ran off.'

'What else did you see?'

'Nothing.'

'Look, this is important, Terry.'

'I wasn't supposed to be there.'

Fear clouded his face. Fear of losing his exclusive right to plunder balls among the trees. Fear of violent men who committed a serious crime by daylight. Fear of the consequences.

'This is strictly between us,' I assured him.

'I didn't see anything, Alan! Honest!'

'You must have heard something.'

'Oh yeah. But only …'

'Go on.'

'They were trampling through the trees.'

'And?'

'There was this little scream then a real charge through the undergrowth. They didn't hang about. By the time I got close enough to see, you were being driven off in a golf buggy by this chauffeur bloke.'

'So what did you do?'

'Went back to the hedge as fast as I could.'

'Hedge?'

'Where we sneak in. I was too late.'

'Why?'

'This van was tearing off down the lane. Couldn't see who was in it but they were certainly in a hurry.'

'Can you describe the van?'

He licked his lips and gave a scared smile.

'I took a photo.'

'Marvellous! Where is it?'

'Film's gone to be developed. Ready tomorrow.'

'Can I have that photo?'

Fear crept in again. Terry Kelso had a much-loved dog and a harmless hobby that gave him a lot of pleasure. He wanted nothing to threaten his little world. Though he was not certain what had happened at Greenblades that morning, he sensed there was big trouble and wanted to be no part of it. He spread his hands apologetically.

'Can't help you,' he said. 'Way I am. Darlo can be a pretty nasty place at times. You see things you wish you hadn't, then the police come calling. I learned to keep my mouth shut. Stay well clear. Safest way.'

'I'll pay you for it, Terry.'

He was tempted. I gave him time to think it over.

'How much?'

'A hundred dollars.'

'For a snapshot of a dirty old van?'

'It's worth that to me,' I said. 'Tell you what, I'll even

101

toss in a bag of dog biscuits for Sheba.'

'You're on, mate!'

'Fine. I'll call round tomorrow.'

'One thing, though,' he insisted. 'Once I give you the snap, that's it. I don't want to get drawn in. And I don't want to know what this is all about.'

'It's a deal.'

I let him give me a guided tour of the golf balls then persuaded him to show me his private entrance to the golf course. It was not a long walk from the house. Sheba came with us and padded on ahead. Terry brought a torch. We turned into a secluded lane that ran down the side of Greenblades. Security at the club was good. For most of the way, a high perimeter fence had been built and topped with barbed wire. At one point, however, it abutted into a thick and prickly hedge. Nature was allowed to provide the protective screen.

Sheba ran to a part of the hedge and vanished from sight. When we reached the spot, I saw there was a hole through which she had gone. Terry bent down, exerted pressure with his shoulder and the gap opened up. I squeezed through and he followed me. Sheba could be heard prancing about nearby. When the torch picked her out, she was standing beside a hollow that had been scooped out of the ground. Terry directed the beam of the torch into the hollow and cackled. Four more golf balls lay there like new-laid eggs in a makeshift nest.

'One of those is mine,' I guessed.

'Sheba slips off on her own sometimes. Does a bit of hunting by herself. I've taught her to put the balls here so that all I have to do is to come and pick 'em up.' He clicked his fingers and the dog bounded over to him to get a congratulatory pat. 'Good girl, Sheba! Good girl!'

We went back out into the lane and I thanked him

for all his help. Refusing another offer of a drink, I waved him off and watched the two of them walk away. Sheba's tail was still threshing madly as they merged with the darkness.

I set off quickly along the boundary fence with my eye on the barbed wire. The light was poor and the lane a trifle eerie but I persevered. After a couple of hundred yards, I found what I was after. The barbed wire had been cut and it had coiled back. We were directly off to the left of the sixteenth fairway. A small ladder or a rope would have got three people over the fence. I winced as I imagined Diane Reinhold being forced over it on the return journey. She would have been shown no courtesies.

I stood there for some time trying to reconstruct the action. They had chosen a good spot for the kidnap. It was not overlooked and they were able to make a speedy getaway. I was still puzzling it out when I heard tyres crackling over the road surface. A large car was rolling soundlessly towards me with its lights off. As I turned to face it, the full beam was switched on and I was pinned against the fence by the glare.

The driver lowered the window to speak to me. The voice was familiar but not at all friendly.

'What are you doing here, Alan?'

It was Lee Whitfield.

The taxi driver who took me back to my hotel was quiet and obliging. He drove in silence and left the interior light on so that I could open the envelope that Clive had given me. I leafed through the photostats and was gripped at once. Rod Melville had not been exaggerating. If the camera was to be trusted, Beverly Nashe had the glittery beauty of a Hollywood film star. Her hair was dark and shoulder-length, her face was set off by high cheekbones and careful make-up, her clothes were exotic. She was a woman who wanted to be noticed and who took full advantage of the attention. In the captions to the photographs, Beverly was described variously as a wife, socialite, magazine editor, television celebrity and star. For all his bulk and black-bearded authority, Warren Oxley was not an impressive figure beside her. Though he was always beaming happily at the camera, it was his first wife who hogged the picture.

Oxley himself was well-documented. His rise had been steady, then sudden, then quite meteoric. There'd been some occasional setbacks – including losses in legal battles against certain firms – but he had powered his way on. His empire was enormous. He had a major stake in oil, coal and aluminium. But it was from launching a series of aggressive takeovers that he really made his reputation. Over a period of three years, he spearheaded no less than fifty-eight hostile bids that helped to boost his profits during that time to well over A$190 million. I noted that his shopping list included newspapers, magazines and some publishing houses.

Warren Oxley wanted to influence opinion.

The more recent the photographs of him, the more distinguished was the company in which he was standing. He was seen with Republican senators in Washington, with leading industrialists in Frankfurt, with ministers in Tokyo and with the chairman of the CBI in London. His operation was becoming increasingly global. In Australia itself, he was often shown in the company of prominent members of the Liberal Party. Perhaps because of his first wife, he also liked to rub shoulders with the stars of the showbiz world and frequented their haunts. It was a remarkable career for the son of a sponge diver from Greece. He exemplified the spirit of his new country.

What surprised me was how few photographs there were of him and Diane Reinhold. While the camera was ever-present during his first marriage, it seemed to have run out of film for the second. There were some shots of the wedding and a fleeting glimpse of the couple at some function but that was all. He and Beverly Nashe lived in public. His second marriage was an altogether more private affair. I put the two wives side by side on my knee to compare them. In terms of instant dazzle, there was no contest. Beverly was the clear winner. But she was essentially an indoor person, a desk-bound operator who thrived in the hothouse of magazine journalism, a media creature whose studied beauty was at its best in the lights of a television studio.

Diane Reinhold, by contrast, was an outdoor girl with a much more natural look. You could see it in her skin, her eyes, her body language. Beverly might be streetwise and shrewd but her rival, I now learned, had two degrees and spent a couple of years in the outback doing research on some project. My acquaintance with her was brief but she had a sense of independence that I admired. Given the choice between the two women, Clive Phelps, along with most other men, would have stripped off and dived straight at the more alluring charms of Beverly Nashe. I preferred Diane Reinhold. There was more poise and quality. She was still too reminiscent of Rosemary for me actually to like her but I missed her intensely. And I cared deeply about the grim situation she was in.

When Oxley married Beverly Nashe, he acquired yet another attractive property: when he met Diane Reinhold, he found a real wife. At a stroke, he changed from glitter to depth. I asked myself why.

The question was still unanswered when we drew up outside the Hilton. The taxi driver lifted my things out of the boot and smirked at my generous tip. As he drove away, I stood on the pavement and pondered. Press cuttings could only tell me so much. What I wanted was inside information. I needed a friend in the Oxley camp.

She was waiting for me inside the hotel.

'Alan! I'm glad I caught you.'

'Hello, Jan.'

'I just dropped off a copy of the Press handout. I thought you ought to know what we've been saying about you.'

'That's very considerate. Have you got time for a drink or something?'

'Why not? I've signed off for another day.'

'Does Oxley push you?'

'Like a slave-driver.'

Jan Cummings smiled but there was a tension around her mouth. She was dressed in a green trouser suit and carried a slimline executive briefcase. Her arrival was just the bonus I needed after my abrasive meeting with Lee Whitfield. It would be restful to share a glass of wine with that red hair and those freckles.

I left my golf bag in reception and conducted her to the bar. We found a quiet corner and ordered drinks from the waitress. Jan still had that professional sheen to her but I sensed her visit might be of a more personal nature. As we stayed in neutral gear and chatted about my first impressions of Greenblades, I began to wonder if she had been planted on me. Lee Whitfield had not believed my story about having gone for a walk down that lane. It would have been easy for him to ring from his car and alert Oxley to the fact that I was disobeying orders and sniffing. Jan Cummings might well be the result of that phone conversation.

I decided to find out by the most direct method.

'Why did you come here tonight?'

'To drop off the Press release.'

'That wasn't important enough to bring you over here at this time of night,' I said. 'Besides, you could have faxed it through to me. How long have you been waiting?'

'I'd just walked through the door.'

'Does Oxley know that you're here?'

'No.'

'Mind if I ring him and check that?'

Her hand moved out involuntarily to hold my arm as I made to rise. The gesture was eloquent. Far from being a plant, she was keen that her visit was kept a secret from her employer. I relaxed and sat back down again.

Jan crossed her legs and leaned forward.

'I wanted to speak to you, Alan.'

'That's more like it.'

'This is in strictest confidence, mark you.'

'My lips are sealed.'

'It's Diane.'

'What about her?'

'I'm hoping that you can tell me.'

'Oh?' I played dumb.

'Something's happened to her.'

'Why do you think that?'

'Because nobody seems to know where she is. I've tried everywhere I can think of but to no avail. She's vanished into thin air.'

'What does her husband say?'

'Very little and that's a dead giveaway. He likes to ring her every day at some time. Just to touch base. Not today. Warren's been edgy which is not like him.'

'Maybe she's run off with her secret lover.'

'Don't joke about it.'

Inwardly, I chided myself. The two men who spirited Diane away at the golf course did so with force. They were anything but secret lovers and I felt a sharp

107

stab of regret as I heard what I said. It did not seem to show in my face. Jan was still fishing.

'You must have been the last person to see her.'

'Why?'

'She came to Greenblades this morning.'

'Acted as my caddie. Extremely good at the job.'

'And afterwards?'

'We just parted company. I came back here.'

'Did Diane say where she was going?'

'I didn't ask her, Jan.'

'Oh.' She bit her lip. 'What time did you leave?'

'Not long after noon.'

'You didn't see Warren by any chance?'

'No.'

'What about Lee?'

'Sorry.'

'Where did they go, then?' She fondled her glass pensively and looked up at me. 'I was in the office when Warren took a call. It was short and sweet. He and Lee then went out quickly. I just can't fathom it.'

Jan Cummings allowed her surface calm to crack slightly and it made her much more appealing. I have never been very fond of that hard-edged femininity that seems to be in vogue these days. If women – or men, for that matter – want to be assertive, they can go and do it over someone else. I usually switch off. But a hint of weakness is guaranteed to switch me back on again as it did now. If she could show her vulnerability, it meant that she trusted me. And if she trusted me, whom she had known for just over twenty-four hours, then she obviously had nobody else to whom she could turn.

We sipped our drinks and communicated wordlessly for a few minutes. Without any effort, we were drawn more closely together. When I'm involved in a golf tournament, I have one golden rule. No emotional entanglements. They only distract me from the matter in hand and I usually need all my concentration. But rules are made to be broken and these circumstances were rather special. To begin with, it was not a four-day tournament against a large field. I'd be one of a quartet playing thirty-six holes. Even if I finished last in the money race, I'd make a minimum of £40,000. In any case, I was willing to throw away every penny of it in favour of helping Diane and an alliance with Jan Cummings would be one way of doing that. I love golf and the fat cheques it can sometimes earn but there are higher considerations.

Diane was one of them. I wanted my caddie back.

Simple biology was also at work. Jan liked me and I now realised just how much I liked her. My love life had been barren and disappointing for some time. Rosemary's announcement had exacerbated my depression. Here was a wonderful diversion, sitting only a couple of feet away, giving me what I hoped were all the right signals. We had mutual needs. If we pooled our resources, we would not be the only ones to gain from it.

It had been a long, tiring, testing day.

Jan Cummings was the best thing in it.

'Do you like working for Warren Oxley?' I said.

'No.'

'What do you think of Lee Whitfield?'

'He makes my flesh creep.'

'Who is he?'

'A crook.'

It was just what I wanted to hear. Honest, direct and reassuringly disloyal. She was making a commitment. It was the moment for me to do the same but I could not get my tongue around the words. Whether it was fatigue or guilt or fear of rejection I don't know, but I held back and scolded myself for doing so. It was excruciating.

Jan Cummings put me out of my misery.

'Let's go up to your room,' she said.

Australia was starting to deliver at last.

It was my first consignment of luck.

CHAPTER FOUR

LIFE IS A CONTINUING PROCESS of discovery. No matter what your age or your breadth of experience, there's always something new around the corner. Until that night at the Hilton, I had no conception of how enjoyable it could be to share a whirlpool bath with a gleaming woman. I was amazed at what could be achieved in swirling, warm water by two people with a common purpose. Four long legs and the desire to blot out the real world gave our union both spice and urgency. We floated in a time capsule that took us light years away from our problems. In the liquid joy of it all, we almost persuaded ourselves that we loved each other. It was exquisite.

Alan, Alan. Jan, Jan. Alan, Jan. Jan, Alan.

Rosemary? Who was she?

Memory was kind. It kept cynicism at bay. It gave us the illusion that the moment could last for eternity, that the hot deeds of night would never have to submit to the cold light of day, that we were somehow fulfilling our destiny. Nothing disturbed us. All was harmony. There were no discordant notes, no strident reminders of just how ephemeral it really was. We indulged ourselves.

Naked, wet and deliciously exhausted, we lay on the bed together to recover. The afterglow was another form of intoxication. We grew closer, lost inhibitions and lowered our guards. Dangers were scorned. Whole hours seemed to glide past. Had we achieved nirvana?

'Alan?'

'Mm?'

'Are you awake?'

'I hope not.'

'Tell me about Diane.'

'Who?'

'Something terrible has happened to her.'

'Come back to sleep.'

'You know what it is.'

I rolled over to lie on top of her and ran my fingers through the flame-red hair. When I tried to kiss her, she stopped me and looked up pleadingly.

'I want to be told.'

'Diane has been kidnapped.'

Shock hit her like a blow then she burst into tears. I comforted her as best I could and found her a tissue to dab at her eyes. Sitting up against the headboard, she made an effort to control herself and pressed for the details. I gave her an edited version of events that stopped at the point where Warren Oxley warned me off. Terry Kelso and his dog belonged solely to me.

The mood had now darkened. Delirium in the whirlpool bath had been replaced by despair in the bedroom. The plug had been pulled and the water had run out.

'We must help her, Alan!' she urged.

'How?'

'There's got to be something we can do.'

'Oxley wants to handle it alone.'

'Diane is my friend.'

'She was my caddie.'

Jan suddenly seemed to be cold. She gave a shiver, wrapped her arms around herself and hopped out of bed.

'Could I have a coffee, please?'

'Room service or home-made?'

'Instant will do.'

While I filled the kettle under one of the bathroom taps, Jan came in to borrow the white robe from the back of the door. She was now *distraite*. I felt compelled to put on my pyjama trousers and the name of Rosemary began to mean something to me again. Sanity was back. I made two coffees and handed one to Jan who was now sitting in front of the dressing table. She waved away my offer of milk and sugar. I rested on the edge of the bed.

Admonition made her turn to face me.

'How could you, Alan?'

'How could I what?'

She shrugged. 'All this ...'

'You asked me. I wanted it. Lift-off!'

'But you knew.'

'Yes, I did.'

'You knew that Diane was in that dreadful situation and yet you went ahead as if ...' Reproof put a hardness in her eye. 'What sort of a man are you?'

'Regulation issue. Flesh and blood.'

'If I'd realised that Diane was —'

'But you didn't,' I interrupted, crossing over to her. 'And you wouldn't have found out if we hadn't come up here together. There's no way I would have confided in you otherwise. I had to be sure I could trust you, Jan. Let's face it. I didn't have to admit anything at all.'

'That's true.'

'Besides,' I continued, 'what happened between us was much more than just a testing procedure. I felt so, anyway. I hoped you did.'

She thought about it and nodded. I knelt down and put my hands on her shoulders. Jan Cummings stroked my cheek absent-mindedly with the back of her hand and sampled her coffee. Our moment had passed. It was time to turn all our attention to Diane Reinhold.

I got up, took my own coffee and paced the room.

'Okay,' I said. 'Let's make a list.'

'Of what?'

'Suspects.'

She sighed. 'It won't be that easy, Alan.'

'Why not?'

'There are so many.'

'That's a problem.'

'Warren is good at making enemies. He almost revels in it. There are dozens of people who'd just love to take a crack at him.'

'Such as?'

'Businessmen he's ruined. Politicians he's used and cast aside. Employees he's sacked. Then, of course, there's the unions. They hate him.'

'And Diane?'

'What about her?'

'Did she have lots of enemies as well?'

'No,' she said firmly. 'Diane isn't like him. She knows what real friendship means. Everybody likes her.'

'Including Beverly Nashe?'

'That's different.'

'Could she be involved in this?'

'I don't know. I doubt it.'

'In that case, someone kidnapped Diane to get at her husband. Or his filthy lucre. Any guesses?'

She shook her head. I changed my tack.

'Tell me about Lee Whitfield.'

'We don't get on.'

'You called him a crook.'

'I was being polite.'

'Is he Oxley's right-hand man?'

'The knee-kicker.'

'Come again.'

'Lee's own word for himself,' she explained. 'His father used to be a carpet-layer. He and Warren are two of a kind. Always boasting about their humble origins as if it's some kind of credential. Sons of a carpet-layer and a sponge-diver. I never mention that my father's a bank manager. That would be a black mark against me.'

'What's a knee-kicker?'

'A heavy steel device they use to flatten everything out. When they lay a fitted carpet, they kick this thing across it with their knees to iron out any lumps or wrinkles. That's what Lee Whitfield does.'

'Keeps everything smooth on the surface.'

'Exactly,' she said bitterly. 'When they take over a new company, Lee is sent in to get rid of any lumps. He's an expert. If there's any protest or opposition, the knee-kicker always does the trick. Legally or otherwise.'

'Nice man!'

'Don't get on the wrong side of him, Alan.'

'I think I already have.' I sat on the bed again and looked at her fondly. 'Why do you put up with it, Jan?'

'With what?'

'Working with people you don't like.'

'It wasn't like this at the start. PA to Warren Oxley. It seemed like a marvellous break.'

'Then you saw him in his true light.'

'Only too clearly.'

'Why don't you just leave?'

'Warren won't let me.'

'But it's your right.'

'I know too much. He'd stop me.'

'How?'

'Lee Whitfield.'

I could see her dilemma. To the outside oberver, she

was a successful young woman in a highly-paid job. But she had too many scruples to approve of the methods that Warren Oxley used. Unfortunately, he did not allow anybody to resign from his employ. They were either dismissed or retained at his decision. Trapped in a corner like that, Jan Cummings would have special reason to appreciate the friendship of Diane Reinhold. It was probably the factor which made the job tolerable.

'How long have you worked for Oxley?'

'Three years.'

'So you know his first wife.'

'Oh, yes!'

'Is she still in Sydney?'

'Very much so.'

'How could I get to see her?'

'By switching on the telly. Beverly Nashe has a chat show three nights a week.'

'And if I wanted to meet her in person?'

'That might not be wise, Alan.'

'But if I did?'

'I'll give you her number.'

'Thanks. Is she really such a knockout?'

'Depends on your taste.'

'I'm looking at mine right now.'

A pale smile. 'I can't compete with Beverly.'

'Diane Reinhold did.'

'She's special.'

'In what way?'

'Only Warren could tell you that.'

'We're not on those terms.'

'Be thankful.'

'Why did he leave his first wife?'

'She tried to kill him.'

Jan Cummings kept her bathrobe on in bed. I removed my pyjama trousers. It was a mistake to try to make love

116

to her again. When I finally dozed off, I woke almost at once with a start.

'She's been kidnapped.'

'Diane?'

'Rosemary.'

'Who?'

'And Lynette.'

'What are you talking about, Alan?'

The voice nagged at me until I came to my senses, laughed it off and settled down again, but the realisation gnawed away at me. My ex-wife and daughter were being kidnapped by David Ridger. What made the crime so traumatic for me was that they were such willing hostages. Diane Reinhold was taken by force and would be held to ransom. Rosemary and Lynette had let themselves be driven off in a new Jaguar and they would spurn any rescue by my chequebook. I was oppressed by the parallels until sleep came to save me.

When I woke again at six o'clock, Jan Cummings had gone. All she left behind was a wistful memory and the telephone number of Beverly Nashe. Somewhere along the line, I botched the relationship. I hoped it could be retrieved. A hot shower and a Continental breakfast revived me and sent me back for a second look at the material that Clive had provided. Studied in better light and at more leisure, it was very revealing. Warren Oxley had a clever public relations consultant. The right image was projected in every photograph or article. No sign of enemies or lumps in the carpet. All was smiling concord.

What I did notice for the first time, however, was the lurking presence of Lee Whitfield. He worked himself into nearly all of the most recent pictures, always on the edge of the action but watching it with interest. When I went back through the photostats, I found that he did not feature in any of the early material. He came into the frame at a specific point some three years ago. Having got in, Lee Whitfield stayed there. All over Australia there must be people with carpets laid by his father.

I was glad that I was not one of them.

Vic collected me at the appointed time and drove me to Greenblades. He chatted volubly to cover his unease. The kidnap had turned an affable man into a neurotic. He kept glancing up at the rear-view mirror again as if expecting to see the knee-kicker in pursuit.

It was another sunny day. As we crossed the Harbour Bridge, I saw from the sails down below that wind was going to be a problem again. Herm Wexler was right about the course. It was a gorilla. On a windy day, a huge club was put into its hand. It was armed and dangerous.

'Any news of the betting, Vic?'

'On what?'

'The game.'

'Oh, that.'

'How am I doing?'

'Second favourite.'

'After?'

'Gil Jericho.'

My heart sank. I'd conveniently forgotten Gil Jericho and I was jolted by the sound of his name. The prospect of having to play golf with him again was a lowering one and seemed at that moment to be the crowning misfortune. Assault with chloroform. Kidnap. Strong arm stuff from Oxley. Confrontation with Lee Whitfield. A fatal tactical error with Jan Cummings. Now this.

Come on, Australia. Where's my luck?

I remembered Terry Kelso and rallied somewhat. He was the one redeeming aspect of it all, the ray of

118

hope in an otherwise black sky. An amiable old character with an eccentric hobby might yet give me a vital clue. There was little enough to go on so far. Most of the evidence was confusing or contradictory.

I pinned everything on one man and his dog.

Greenblades was transformed. In place of the empty country club I had entered at the same time on the previous day was a sort of *al fresco* Bedlam. Working since dawn, an army of men had erected towers for the television cameras and hospitality tents for the privileged visitors. Miles of cable snaked everywhere. Canvas flapped like a Spanish Armada. Advertisers attacked from hoardings or banners. As the principal sponsor, Warren Oxley had his name fluttering on a white flag above the clubhouse. Catering supplies were being unloaded from large vans. Temporary staff were being instructed in their duties. There was an air of civilised pandemonium about the whole scene.

Journalists added to the chaos. Equipped with what looked like two or three photographers each, they lay in wait outside the locker room for the first arrivals. I was besieged as soon as I got out of the car and had to give a dozen simultaneous interviews as I made my way to the clubhouse. Most of them followed me through into the locker room. One – who came to regret it – tried to accompany me to the toilet.

It was half an hour before I could shake myself clear and get on the first tee. There was one boon. His name was Frank Davey and he was my caddie.

'Ignore the buggers,' he said cheerfully.

'Just tell me how.'

'They're like flies around a cow's arse.'

'What shall I swat them with?'

'Try a 5-iron. Plenty of wrist.'

Frank Davey was a short, stout, swarthy man in his forties with leathery skin and a dry sense of humour.

Wearing a red, white and blue T-shirt that had my name on its back, he took a relaxed attitude to the whole thing. After a couple of holes, I sensed that I might have struck gold. Frank knew every inch of the course and talked about it with offhand fondness. He was supportive and imaginative. He knew when to be invisible and when to make his presence felt. I could rely on him.

He got me out of a sticky situation at the third.

'How're you feeling?' he said.

'Much better.'

'Don't let Greenblades scare you.'

'I won't.'

'You must win the pot.'

'Why?'

'I need the money.'

His deadpan delivery was a tonic in itself. I still missed Diane Reinhold as my caddie but Frank Davey was an ideal substitute. Moreover, he would complete the round. His Popeye the Sailor forearms would deter any kidnap attempts on the sixteenth green. In every sense, I was safe with him. I could give myself to my game.

The course was as unyielding as ever but the novelty of its terrors had worn off. Even with the wind as its accomplice, it produced no spinal shivers. Greenblades was there for the man bold enough to take it. Guile was no solution. Patience was not the prime requisite. It was with a display of attacking golf that it would be tamed.

'Let's go for it, Frank.'

'Suits me.'

'Route Number One. No frills.'

'That's what I like to hear.'

Counselled by my caddie, I took a more adventurous approach. I hit zooming drives, I soared over treetops,

I spanned turbulent water like the Harbour Bridge. From every lie and every angle, I attacked the pin. We had our share of catastrophe but it did not check me. I hooked, I sliced, I nose-dived into sand, I went out of bounds and I lost a ball on the fourteenth but I still maintained my frontal assault. Oblivious to the knot of golf writers and spectators who trailed me, I powered my way to the eighteenth hole. Greenblades might not have been conquered but I'd certainly dented its pride. When I sank my final putt of the round, I had a sense of triumph.

It was smothered beneath a familiar whine.

'The greens are too bloody slick.'

'Hello, Gil.'

'And what about those pin placements? Lethal!'

'Same for all four of us.'

'I'm lodging a formal complaint.'

'Frightened?'

'Of course not,' he said. 'But there are limits. The only way I'd want to go round Greenblades is at the wheel of a bloody bulldozer. First thing I'd do is fill in some of those bunkers at the opening hole. It's like a replica of the Gibson Fucking Desert. I mean to say, we're professional golfers – not flaming camels!'

I could have disputed his right to the title but I let it pass. Gil Jericho was no professional golfer. He was a hustler with a corrupted talent. There are few games that lend themselves so readily to the cheat and to the liar. It is virtuously impossible to eradicate them completely. They flourish best at club level among the gullible and the well-intentioned, but the occasional villain does slip into the professional game. Gil Jericho was one of them. Standards of honesty are remarkably high on the circuits with golfers frequently admitting to errors that cost them strokes and money. Jericho would admit nothing. If he could get away with something, he would try it. A flick of the foot to improve his lie, an unreported air shot, an extra few inches when he replaced his ball on a marker – these were standard ploys. Too cunning to be caught, he varied his techniques relative to the vigilance of his playing partners and the officials.

'Nice to see you again, Al,' he said

'I can't return the compliment.'

He laughed. 'You're not still sore about Turnberry?'

'I like a fair fight.'

'That's what you got.'

'Not from you.'

'Check the record books. I won that tournament.'

'No comment.'

He laughed again. Gil Jericho was a slight man of middle height with a need to be noticed. He always dressed in black and wore his dark hair down to his shoulders. A pencil moustache gave a spivvy look to a thin face that looked older than its thirty years. I saw that his caddie sported a T-shirt with the colours of the Australian flag. His country could have chosen a more honourable representative than Gil Jericho.

He sidled across for a more private chat.

'I hear you had wrist trouble.'

'Better now.'

'What happened – she close her legs too sudden?'

'You've got a foul mind, Gil.'

'Years of practice.'

'Pity it wasn't spent on a golf course.'

'That's not very friendly,' he complained.

'Did you expect it to be?'

'I thought we were mates.'

'After Turnberry?'

A shoulder-shrugging smirk. 'Don't you think it's time you put Turnberry behind us? It was centuries ago. Besides, I came out as clean as a whistle.'

'Not on my scorecard.'

'You ratted on me: I was exonerated.'

'It's my duty to report unfair play.'

'But there wasn't any.'

'They'll catch up with you one day, Gil.'

'My conscience is clear.'

'I didn't know you had one.'

He winked. 'Enjoy it in the Loser's Enclosure.'

'Don't write me off too soon.'

'Move over, old timer. Your era is past.'

'At least I had one.'

'My memory doesn't go back that far.'

'I fancy my chances at Greenblades.'

'Yes, you should finish in the top four.'

'Wish I could say the same for you, Gil.'

'My name's already on the winning cheque.'

'You obviously haven't spotted the cameras,' I said. 'They'll watch your every move in close-up. We're being televised here. Not like Turnberry.'

He laughed, slapped me on the shoulder and walked away with his caddie. The tragedy was that Gil Jericho could have been a superb golfer if he had worked hard at his game instead of at his gamesmanship, but that would have been to deny his essence. He had a devil-may-care streak which obliged him to sail close to the wind and his success rate was appreciable. Although he had been fined three times and warned about conduct unbecoming to a professional golfer, he stayed firmly in the game and even more firmly in the money.

'That it for the day?' said Frank.

'No.'

'Good.'

'Five o'clock?'

'I'll be around.'

'How long have you been a caddie?'

'Too long.'

'Ever carried a bag for Gil Jericho?'

'Only once. At the Royal.'

'How did you get on with him?'

'He pays well.'

'As a person, I meant.'

'Okay.'

'Is he straight?'

'Don't buy a second-hand club off him.'

Frank said it all. We went back to the locker room.

I was surrounded once again for comments about the course and for predictions about the big event. It was some time before I could escape to the clubhouse to buy Frank a drink while we sorted out our financial arrangements. Members had been banned from playing for the day and there were some mutinous comments from those who resented standing aside to give the four of us unlimited access and to allow the greenkeepers to put the final touches to the course. I got the strong impression that the Warren Oxley circus was not entirely welcome.

With Frank's help, I'd been able to lose myself totally in my golf and that was an encouraging sign. Now, however, my mind turned back to Diane Reinhold. She was in grave danger and I might be able to help. That was paramount. I made my farewell, left the clubhouse and went towards the drive. But when I reached the angle of the building, I saw something that made me stop in my tracks.

In the car park, standing beside a silver BMW, were two figures in earnest conversation. Something about their manner suggested that they were close friends. I was certain that they were not discussing golf. After a few minutes, they got into the car and drove quickly away.

Birds of a feather. Two men I freely despised.

Gil Jericho and Lee Whitfield.

During my walk the previous evening, I'd noticed the run of shops in an adjacent road. There was no pet shop and so I trusted to Noonan's Mini Market. They came through with a box of dog biscuits and it rattled invitingly. I was sure that Sheba would be grateful. She'd earned it. I strolled on to the crescent of bungalows and went up to the one owned by Terry Kelso. It looked almost habitable in daylight. The doorbell failed to bring him and even a pounding on the glass panel fell on deaf ears. Yet I was certain that he was at home. I peered in through the window of the living room to find it empty. Making my way around to the bedroom, I peeped in through a gap in the curtains and got a profound shock.

The treasured collection of golf balls had gone.

They had been hacked from the wall and taken away. Debris lay all over the floor. It was a scene of utter devastation, made all the more poignant by the object that lay on the bed. It was Sheba's collar.

The noise alerted me. Terry was in the garden. I could hear a spade doing its work with sharp thrusts. When I went around the back of the house, I saw him in his shirtsleeves, breathing hard and sweating in the hot sun, digging a deep hole so that he could shovel the golf balls into it. It was not the only hole he had dug that day. Beside it was a mound of freshly-turned earth and I knew at once who lay beneath it. Sheba was beyond dog biscuits now. She had been killed in cold blood. Terry Kelso had lost all interest in golf. He was burying his past.

There was no point in asking for the photograph of the van. It had been taken. I left quietly and stuffed the hundred dollars through his letterbox. The box of biscuits was discarded in the bin outside the shops. My guilt was leaden. Because of me, an old man had been ruthlessly separated from the creature he loved most. I was hopelessly late.

Someone got there first.

Vic took me back to the Hilton where I went straight up to my room. I let myself in to be greeted by yet another unpleasant sight. He was sitting calmly in an armchair.

'Hello, Alan. Come on in?'

'What the hell are you doing here?'

'Waiting for you.'

'This is my room!'

'I'm paying for it.'

'That doesn't give you the right to barge in.'

'Calm down.'

'I'll move out today.'

Warren Oxley was wearing a cream suit with a yellow flower in his buttonhole. I was furious at the intrusion. He sat there with fleshy composure. It was galling.

'Don't you like the suite?'

'I loved it – until now.'

'Stay here as long as you like.'

'So that you can drop in on me?'

'It may not be necessary again.'

'I'll cancel the reservation,' I said, reaching for the telephone. 'And I'll tell the manager what I think about his room service.'

'It's not his fault. I let myself in.'

'How?'

'Most doors are open to me, Alan,' he said with a rough charm. 'Now put that telephone down. My offer stands. This room is yours for as long as you wish to stay in Sydney. All expenses paid.' I slowly replaced the receiver. 'That's better.'

'What do you want?'

'Absolute privacy. This was the best place.'

'Have you had a thorough search?'

'Don't stand on your dignity.'

126

'You forced your way into my —'

'What happens to Diane is much more important than your hurt feelings,' he said emphatically. 'I came to talk about her. When I need to do something, I make up my own rules. Is that clear?'

I bit back my protest and nodded reluctantly. He jabbed a finger towards a chair but I ignored the instruction and remained standing. He clicked his tongue and shook his head.

'You're not very good at doing what you're told.'

'I have this hatred of authority figures.'

'We'll have to cure you of that.' He stood up and ambled across to me. 'Why did you disobey me?'

'Because I wanted to help Diane.'

'And you think that you can do that on your own?'

'It was worth a try.'

He put his hand in his pocket and took out a small photograph. After glancing at it, he handed it to me and I saw a picture of an old van with a ladder strapped to its roof rack. The vehicle was shot from behind as it raced away down the lane. The numberplate was hard to read.

'Go on,' he urged. 'Try. Help my wife.'

'It'll take time.'

'She hasn't got time.'

'In that case, I'll —'

'Save yourself the trouble,' he said, snatching the photograph from me. 'We've already checked it out. That van belongs to a firm that puts up television aerials. They're as anxious to trace it as we are. It was stolen from outside their premises in Surrey Hills. How long would it have taken you to find that out?'

'Did you have to kill his dog?'

'The old man was stubborn.'

'Who did it – Whitfield?'

'Sit down, Alan.'

Before I could resist, he pushed me into a chair and stood over me. When I tried to get up, he forced me down again without effort. In a trial of strength, he was to come off best. Warren Oxley called the tune.

'Don't fail me again,' he said.

'Is that what I did?'

'You failed Diane as well.'

'That wasn't deliberate.'

'I told you to keep out of it but you were much too inquisitive, weren't you? All right, mate, we'll play it your way. If you want a piece of the action, you're in.'

'What do you mean?'

'They've contacted me again.'

'The kidnappers?'

'They're ready to trade. One million dollars.'

'Is Diane safe?'

'I spoke to her. She's safe enough.'

'What will you do?'

'Pay it.'

'No police?'

'None of their business.'

'So you just give in?'

'I want my wife back. The money is of no concern to me. They're welcome to it. The trade will take place on Saturday night. They'll give me precise details nearer the time. All I know is that someone must take the cash to them in used notes and get Diane in exchange.'

'Why are you telling me this?'

'You're that someone.'

I got through to her on the telephone at once and she agreed to see me without any prevarication. During the taxi ride to the studios, I had the chance to take on board the enormity of my commission from Warren Oxley. I was to be the go-between. It was not a role that I relished and I kept thinking of all those gangster films in which the middle man is always seen as an expendable item. At the same time, however, it would lend a symmetry to the whole thing. Diane was forcibly taken away from me and I was the person to whom she would be returned. If the kidnappers honoured their side of the bargain, that is. I had doubts there. On balance, I wanted someone else to do the job but I could see why Oxley had selected me.

I had more or less asked for it.

The studio was a large, nondescript building of red brick in its own grounds. I was expected. A young woman showed me to a viewing room and left me alone with little more than three chairs and a television monitor. When I glanced at the screen, I saw with horror that it was showing one of the very serials I'd left Britain to escape, one of those glum soap operas that weigh you down with the sheer relentlessness of their trivia then hit you with the upbeat jingle of their theme tune. I switched off as she came into the room.

Beverly Nashe was indeed something special and I wished that I'd arranged to meet her elsewhere. Her personality would have been big enough in an aeroplane hangar. In the confines of a small room, it was positively suffocating. It wasn't just the beauty and the body. It was the whole package – the hair, the careful make-up, the designer clothes, the jewellery, the posture, the husky voice and the false brightness that seems to be the stock-in-trade of television celebrities.

The handshake was a lingering exploration.

'Good of you to call me, Alan,' she said.

'Thanks for seeing me at such short notice.'

'I realised that time was of the essence. You're playing in a golf tournament tomorrow. It's appallingly ignorant of me, I know, but I couldn't tell you what a Skins Game is. I'm not sure that Warren could either.'

'It's about Warren that I came …'

'So you said. What's the problem?'

'Well, I'd like to ask some personal questions.'

She laughed. 'Ask away. I don't embarrass easily.'

Having recovered from her initial impact, I now saw that Beverly Nashe was not quite as imposing a figure as she'd seemed. Her face was spotty, her neck was starting to betray her age and she had a nervous habit of crossing and uncrossing her slender legs. Her expression was a blend of beauty and the basilisk.

'Come on, darling,' she prompted. 'I don't bite.'

'That's disappointing.'

'Plunge straight in. Warren and I were married for six years. I know everything there is to know about him.'

'Do you know why he left you?'

Her nostrils flared. 'I left him.'

'That's not the way I heard it.'

'Then you heard wrong, darling,' she hissed. 'Do I look like the sort of woman a man would walk out on?'

'Not unless he's mad.'

'It was entirely my decision.'

'If you say so.'

'I junked Warren.'

'Why?'

'Because he was getting very boring.'

'Away a lot? Preoccupied with his work?'

'Amongst other things.'

'Such as?'

'I'd seen everything he could do.'

She tossed her hair and struck a pose. Beverly Nashe had rewritten the story of her marriage break-up to suit herself. It was going to be a sticky interview.

'What about Diane Reinhold?' I said.

'What about her?'

'Didn't she come between you?'

'You certainly know how to insult a lady!'

'Sorry, Beverly.'

130

'Reinhold is nothing!'

'Warren did marry her.'

'Sheer desperation. He's regretted it ever since.'

'Has he? How do you know?'

'Because he told me so himself, of course. Reinhold may live with him now but I'm still the one he turns to when the shit hits the fan. I'm number one.'

'You actually see each other?'

'Why shouldn't we?' She studied me through narrowed lids. 'Are you married, Alan?'

'I was.'

'Divorce?' I nodded. 'Whose fault?'

'Both of us.'

'Do you still see your wife?'

'Not if I can help it.'

'Painful memories?'

'Very painful.'

'Do you loathe her that much?'

'It's more a case of fear.'

'She still has the power to hurt you, then?'

'Sometimes.'

'In that case, your wife left you.'

'Yes.'

'It was different with Warren and myself.' She did the leg routine again but I was too busy thinking about Rosemary to enjoy it. 'We did a deal. This for that, that for this. And so on. It worked for six years. Then I realised that I was coming off worst in the deal. In some ways, he pushed me forward but in others he was holding me back. I had my career to think of, after all.'

'When did you leave him?'

'At the start of this year, I suppose.'

'So it was nothing to do with Diane?'

'Who's she?'

Her hard stare was all basilisk and no beauty.

'What about the yacht?' I said.

'He named it after me.'

'Wasn't it burned out?'

'That was very unfortunate.'

'Arson?'

'An electrical fault. I was lucky to escape.'

Beverly Nashe was her own electrical fault. She was liable to cause an explosion at any moment. It was easy to see how a man like Warren Oxley could yield to her attractions but hard to understand how he had weathered them for six years. Sparks flew from her all the time. She was a different order of being from Diane Reinhold. A media harpy with an acid tongue behind the meticulous lipstick.

'Why did you come here?' she demanded.

'To talk about Warren.'

'For what reason?'

'Curiosity.'

'About him or me?'

'Both of you together. The marriage.'

'There's more to it than that.'

'No, there isn't.'

'I know what brought you here.'

'What?'

'You're having an affair with Reinhold.'

I still cannot understand why I blushed but it was all the confirmation she needed. She laughed harshly at what she thought was the betrayal of Warren by his second wife. There was no point in telling her that I'd known Diane for less than twenty-four hours and that her resemblance to Rosemary was too close for comfort. In trying to question Beverly Nashe, I'd given away far more about myself. One thing was certain. This first wife was not responsible for the kidnap of the second. She had already had her revenge on Diane by letting her marry Warren Oxley. That was far worse.

She rose to her feet and dismissed me regally.

'You'll have to excuse me, Alan.'

'Before you go …'

'Well?'

'Did you want to kill Warren?'

'Sometimes.'

'Why?'

'All wives have an occasional urge to murder their husbands. Yours was probably no different.'

'She was – she succeeded.'

'I only really tried that once.'

'What happened?'

'The shot missed him by miles.'

'Deliberately?'

'I wish I knew, Alan.'

'Can you remember why you fired at him?'

'Naturally.'

'Where was it?'

'On the yacht. My yacht with my name on it.' She let her bitterness show through at last. 'I caught him trying to get into bed with one of his PAs.'

'Which one?'

'Jan Cummings.'

It was not easy to disentangle fact from fiction in her account. Beverly Nashe's version of reality was a highly personal one and I had to make allowance for inordinate pride and a lasting anguish. No wife could walk out on Warren Oxley unless he sent her on her way. She was lying about that. On the matter of the attempted killing, she was just as clearly telling the truth. Oxley had been caught with his trousers down. I found myself wishing that it had been with anybody other than Jan Cummings.

Why did I always pick women who let me down?

Or was it they who picked me?

The return journey was far too short a time in which

to sort it all out. When I paid the taxi driver and went into my hotel, I was still grappling with the problems. There was an urgent message for me to ring Clive who was at his hotel. When I got through, he insisted that I came at once. I walked around to the Regent and met him in the bar. The obligatory drink was in front of him and he was puffing at a cigar of Churchillian proportions.

'Put it out,' I ordered.

'I need the consolation of tobacco.'

'Try chewing it. More sociable.' I took the cigar from him and stubbed it out in an ashtray. 'There! I can actually see you now.'

Not that it was a very appetising sight. Clive was showing his usual signs of over-indulgence. His eyes were pouched, his skin was crabby, his moustache had a downward droop. There was a world-weary air to him. I thought I could diagnose his complaint.

'She said no.'

'Worse, Alan. She said yes.'

'So what's the trouble?'

'She asked if she could bring a friend.'

'Ah, I get it,' I said with a chuckle. 'You finally bit off more than you can chew. Face it, Clive. You have to moderate your transports. You just can't handle two any more.'

'Chance would be a fine thing!'

'But you said she brought along a friend.'

'Yes. Because I assumed it would be another woman.'

'It wasn't?'

'Not unless they make 'em with beards and huge, hairy arses down here. He was revolting. Tattoos all over his arms and this medallion around his neck.' Clive turned a glaucous eye on me. 'I'm all for new experiences but this one was above and beyond the call

134

of duty. And talk about hogging the action. He didn't give me a look in. They were banging away like billyho for over an hour with me stood there like a fool wondering if there would be any left over for me.'

'Was there?'

'Oh, yes. But not from her. When I finally got a hand on her tit, she told me she fancied a bath and why didn't I just carry on with Eric? Can you imagine it? Eaten alive by that hairy monster!'

'Must've been a night of madness.'

'It was,' he confessed. 'And the madness was mine. I should never have invited her up there. All she wanted was a place where she could be shagged within an inch of her life by King Kong. It was not a pretty sight. Old Eric did everything but beat on his chest.'

'How did you two make out?' I teased.

'We didn't. I told them both to leave.'

'Did they?'

'Not until they'd had a quickie for the road.' He curled his lip in disdain. 'Sex is a gruesome business. I don't know why I bother with it. Talk about aversion therapy. Those two have put me right off it.'

I laughed my fill then weighed in with a bit of sympathy. Clive had been hoist with his own petard. It was likely to slow him down but only temporarily. As soon as the next girl smiled at him, he would be away. His powers of recovery were impressive.

'So what's the big news?' I said.

'I've just told you.'

'That? You brought me running around here to listen to your bedtime stories?'

'It was a traumatic experience for me.'

'And for Eric. He can't cope with rejection.'

'It was a close call.'

'Sounds hilarious to me.'

'You should try it some time!'

135

'I've got worries enough as it is.'

I told him about Oxley's visit to my room and how I'd been elected as the go-between. I also told him about the visit to Beverly Nashe. He came out of his trance.

'Why didn't you tell me you were going to see her?' he said irritably. 'I'd have gone along with you.'

'She's not into threesomes.'

'Nor am I any more.'

'It was quite an experience.'

'Get much out of her?'

'I haven't decided.'

'Was she cagey?'

'Very.'

'That squares with everything I've heard about her.' He sat up and shook off his nocturnal disappointment. 'I did some more ferreting about Oxley.'

'Any joy?'

'He'd never win a Popularity Contest.'

'Tell me something new.'

'Even his friends admit he's a slippery customer. His enemies – and there are thousands of those – treat him like a notifiable disease. Oxley is not as immune from attack as you might imagine. They had a real go at him last year.'

'Over what?'

'Just about everything. Insider dealing. Fiddling the books. Contravening Federal legislation. They kicked up a big stink about a company he tried to buy in his wife's name – the erstwhile Bev. There was some scandal over financial mismanagement and Oxley had to abort the takeover and get out fast. He really got his fingers burned over that one.'

'When was this?'

'Just before Christmas,' said Clive. 'The New Year didn't bring any happier tidings for him. Oxley's mining operations had the environmentalists hopping like demented kangaroos. They took him to court on a whole range of issues, including river pollution.'

'Did they make the charges stick?'

'Some of them. Oxley got a hefty fine and a stern warning. More bad publicity at a time when he least needed it.'

'What do you mean?'

'Notice anything about that material I gave you?'

'Oxley is moving more in political circles.'

'Exactly,' he said, finishing his drink. 'So he must have the right image. Caring, positive, responsible. No dirty work at the crossroads. No nasty stories about dumping effluent in the nation's water supply. Warren Oxley is ambitious. He's not hobnobbing with politicians for the good of his soul. He wants power. There's talk of grooming him to be the next President of the Liberal Party. Know much about Australian politics?'

'Only that it's not a world for nice people.'

'Don't be fooled by the word Liberal. They're the Conservatives down here. As opposed to the ruling Labour Party under Bob Hawke. The Liberals didn't get much of a look-in during the 1980s but they've worked hard to widen their base. Oxley worked with them. His politics are simple – he's slightly to the right of Adolf Hitler.'

'I see what you're driving at, Clive.'

'Now is the time for all good men to come to the aid of the Party.'

'Scandal and bad publicity at the turn of the year. Beverly's name rolled in the mud. Pressure from his political chums. He was told to clean up his act.'

'That meant cutting down on his night-life. They wanted pictures of him kissing babies, not giving his wife a quick feel at some showbiz party. If he was really going to take off in politics then Beverly Nashe was not the ideal person to have at his side. The Liberal Party doesn't need a spokeswoman on yacht-burning.'

'Warren was better off with someone else.'

'Sober. Academic. Refined.'

'Diane Reinhold.'

There were other factors at work but I felt that we'd stumbled on to the main one. Warren Oxley had had a tempestuous marriage with Beverley Nashe and dumped her when she became a liability. For his second wife, he chose someone who could give him the thing that the first could not provide. Respectability.

Diane Reinhold was part of a whitewash campaign.

'Now for the bad news,' said Clive.

'There's more?'

'You won't like this, Alan.'

'Give it to me straight.'

'Ever heard of Agnew and Pollock?'

'Sounds like a firm of dodgy solicitors.'

'They're publishers. Biggest in Australia.'

'So?'

'Two years ago, they bought out VPC, one of the European giants. It's VPC who've put in a bid for Millward Latimer.'

'Oh.' I saw the implications.

'Millward Latimer is the publishing conglomerate that owns Harvey Jansen Books. That means we're both involved here, old son. You with your autobiography and me with my *Fifty Famous Golfers*.'

'If the takeover goes through …'

'We'll be working for Warren Oxley.'

Greenblades was busier than ever when we got back there. Club members, media people and interested bystanders were everywhere. Herm Wexler was setting out on another round with a small gallery at his heels.

138

Driving balls on the practice hole, Sam Limsong had his own following. A roar in the distance indicated that Gil Jericho was managing to delight his fans. When I was spotted in the car park, I had a fresh pack of journalists on to me. They did their best to coax an injudicious remark out of me.

'Is it true you hate Gil Jericho?'

'Why do you call him a cheat?'

'Are you pursuing a vendetta against him?'

'What's your view of Warren Oxley?'

'Is he good for golf?'

'Any comment on Rod Melville?'

'Don't you like Australians?'

'What have you got against us?'

I ignored it all and made for the locker room. Frank Davey was waiting to let me in while keeping the others out. Clive drifted off to watch the Limsong swing.

'Things're hotting up,' I said.

'Stay cool,' advised Frank.

'Has Gil been priming the Press corps?'

'Probably.'

'He'll try anything to unsettle opponents.'

'Leave him be.'

'I want him out of my hair.'

'Beat him.'

'Let's go.'

As we headed for the first tee, Clive fell in beside me and a clutch of fans dogged our steps. Over to our left, the largest of the hospitality marquees was already in operation. A group of businessmen stood near the open flap, chatting away as they sampled a champagne buffet. Looking after them was a leggy redhead in a mustard suit. Jan Cummings was her usual picture of calm efficiency as she went about her work. Seeing me, she waved a hand and gave a no-regrets-about-what-happened smile that did much to restore my ego. It did not, however, remove the nagging doubt about her that Beverly Nashe implanted in me. Had Jan Cummings really been on intimate terms with Oxley? If so, where did her loyalties now lie? She professed to be a friend of Diane but how deep did that friendship go?

Whose side was she on?

Clive Phelps was on to the by-play in a flash.

'She waved at you.'

'No law against that.'

'She smiled at you. Secretively.'

'It's the effect I have on women.'

'Who is she?' he asked with interest.

'Jan Cummings.'

'What does she do?'

'Works for Oxley. Jan is his PA.'

'If that stands for Priceless Arse, I can see how she got the job. You'll have to introduce me.'

'No chance. She's a nice girl.'

'I need cheering up.'

'Think about your wife and family.'

'Saxon, I'm a man of the world.'

'Then keep yourself pure.'

'Who the hell for?'

'Eric.'

I walked out of range of his expletives.

We spent four valuable hours on the course, charting all its possibilities and putting in extra practice on what we felt could be the key holes. Aided by Frank and supported by my little fan club, I was lost in my game once more. The eighteenth green suddenly loomed up in front of me then it was all over. Each time I played Greenblades, it was a little less intimidating.

As we strolled back towards the clubhouse, the fate of Diane Reinhold was uppermost in my mind again.

The Skins Game had been her inspiration and it was ironic that she would have to miss it. Her love of golf had brought the two of us together and torn us rudely apart. Whatever the dangers, I was the logical person to act as the link between Oxley and the kidnappers.

Frank and I exchanged copious notes in the privacy of the locker room. Now that I'd felt the muscles on the gorilla, I was able to formulate my game-plan to subdue the wild animal. Frank was laconic. He'd weighed me up and saw grounds for cautious optimism. We made a good team. I didn't want to let him or myself down.

The clubhouse bar was a deafening hubbub when we arrived. All my rivals were there. Gil Jericho was talking to Herm Wexler and ploughing new furrows in the latter's forlorn brow. Sam Limsong was sipping an orange juice as he listened to Mary Anne. The three golfers were fine players and I would need to be at the top of my form to hold off their challenge. Whether I could do this – and keep my other problems at bay – remained to be seen.

Jan Cummings was there, a rare female intruder in an otherwise male domain, looking after her guests with that easy sophistication. I was not pleased when she crossed the room to join a thin-faced man with a villainous centre-parting in his hair. Lee Whitfield was the resident hatchet-man. I felt quite certain that he'd disposed of Sheba and I wanted to call him to account for it some time. But not now. I watched Jan smiling at him and wondered if she really detested him as much as she had told me. It was evident that he liked her.

Clive Phelps did not cloak his admiration either.

'She's gorgeous!'

'Behave yourself.'

'Just imagine those long legs wrapped around you.'

I did. It was a stirring memory. I had to stop looking at her. I changed the subject at once.

'You've got some more ferreting to do, Clive.'

'Have I?'

'The man she's with is Lee Whitfield.'

'Lucky sod!'

'Find out what there is between him and Gil Jericho. And do it discreetly. Whitfield could turn nasty.'

'Maybe they're just friends,' he said.

'I've got a hunch it goes deeper than that. They're blood brothers, those two. Clever operators with their eyes on the main chance. I want to know what the pair of them are up to. Okay?'

'Why not find out yourself?'

'I've got an assignation.'

'Having a nibble! I don't believe it.'

'It happens to be the truth,' I admitted. 'I'm going to meet a woman in a motel bedroom.'

'Jan Cummings?'

'Rosemary.'

Vic drove me back to the Hilton so that I could leave my golf bag and change my clothes. My journey into the past began. A brisk walk took me to the Circular Quay where I boarded the Manly Ferry. During our stay in Sydney, we made this same journey across the bay every single day and the experience never palled. Chugging through the water on the Queenscliff gives you the most inspiring view of the city and permits you the leisure to drink it all in. The multi-coloured beauty of Sydney lit up the night sky and I sat out on deck to savour it. A hydrofoil will take you across in half the time – fifteen minutes – but it has nothing like the same surging solidity. The faster crossing suits those in a hurry: the ferry caters for those with time to look and learn and love.

Manly was bright, warm and welcoming. It took me less than five minutes to reach the motel. I was relieved to see that it had not changed at all. It still had the same neon sign that flashed its name out across the bay. Braced for disappointment, I went into reception but that, too, seemed much as I remembered it. Small, neat and cosily modern. The staff still wore those short blue coats with a motel insignia on the breast pocket.

'Can I help you, sir?'

'I hope so.'

'Did you want a room?'

'If it's empty.'

'Single or double?'

'Double. Number twenty-three.'

'Oh. I'm afraid that's taken.'

The receptionist was a well-groomed woman in her thirties. She looked through the booking chart and shook her head apologetically.

'I'm sorry, sir. We could offer you number twenty-one. That's next door. It's identical inside.'

'I'll take it, please.'

'How long will you be staying?'

'An hour at most.'

'An hour?'

'Oh, it's all right,' I soothed. 'I'll pay for the whole night, if need be. This is just a sentimental visit. My wife and I spent a second honeymoon here.'

'Did you enjoy your stay with us?'

'We loved it.'

'Then I'm sure we'll only need to make a token charge,' she said indulgently. 'Under the circumstances. I'll have to clear it with the assistant manager but I'm sure it will be all right.'

'Thanks.'

'What was the name, please?'

'Saxon. Alan Saxon.'

'Excuse me a moment.'

She went off to the office and left me alone to take

stock of nostalgia. The place was even smaller than I recalled but the same oil painting of Ayers Rock stood on the wall. The carved heads had been there in our time as well. Judged by Rosemary's standards, the motel was very cramped and decidedly tacky and yet she never lodged one complaint. Its deficiencies were part of its charm.

The woman came back with a smug smile.

'That will be all right, sir.'

'How much?'

'If you just want to look around – nothing.'

'I'm very grateful.'

'Here's the key.' Her manner changed. 'We would ask you to leave the door open, please.'

'I promise I won't pinch anything.'

'It's not that, sir. You see, we have had this kind of request before. And on one occasion – I believe that gentleman spent his honeymoon here as well – it was very distressing. He'd come back here because his wife had died. The loss was just too much for him to bear ...'

'Suicide?'

She nodded. 'It wasn't good for our business.'

'You won't have to mop up any blood after me.'

My chirpy assurance made her give me a shrewd look but she parted with the key. I went up the narrow staircase to the first floor and noticed a few changes. A fire door now guarded the corridor and appliances were fitted to the wall at regular intervals. The old blue carpet had been replaced by an emerald green one. A sign requested guests to vacate their rooms by noon on the day of departure. Air freshener had been used.

I paused outside number twenty-three, heard voices and moved to the adjacent room. The key led me back into enchantment. Apart from the strong odour of polish, it had not altered one bit. Bed, wardrobe, chairs

144

and dressing table were in the identical position. Motel stationery lay ready. I remembered some of the silly notes we had written to each other on it and wished that I'd kept them. Now that I was here again, in the same building, in a room that was a carbon copy of ours, in a mood that I'd never thought I could recapture, there were several things I wished I'd kept.

Rosemary was one of them.

Pain and pleasure touched me in equal degrees. The agony of lost happiness was balanced by a strange joy. I could understand why I'd loved her and why she felt able to love me. The two of us were alone together. We did not share number twenty-three with the game of golf. I was able to concentrate on her and she was a woman who demanded concentration. I suspected that David Ridger would be good at that. He was a born listener and watcher whereas I was neither when the pressures of my absurd way of life began to tell.

I was a husband among millions. When I stopped looking at my wife, she stopped being there. It was as simple and irrevocable as that.

Crossing to the window, I stared at the fairytale panorama beyond. We had left the curtains open every night so that we could yield to the romance of the view. I stood there for a long time, haunted by regret, lifted by the continuing magic, immersed in memories that had a startling immediacy now that I was back again.

Reality won through. This was a distant outpost in my life and I could not recapture its wonder alone. I did not really want Rosemary back. There had been too many years, marked by too many wounds. There had been too many other women. The things which had brought Rosemary and me together had prised us both apart. I was not for her and she was most definitely not for me. And yet I objected to her proposed marriage. Having nothing to offer myself, I resented the man who did. I was a dog in a manger.

A shudder went through me. I thought it would be a sentimental voyage but it was more akin to the doomed return of a husband after his wife's death. Rosemary was now dead to me. In coming back, I'd not resuscitated our marriage and given it a new lease of life, I'd committed a form of suicide. The bloodless destruction of the man I once was in a motel I once knew.

On impulse, I grabbed the telephone and pressed the call-button. The receptionist answered. She was taken aback by my request but humoured me when I offered to pay for the call. During the long wait, I was able to work out that they must be ten hours or so behind Australian time. That would put them into early afternoon.

The school secretary came on and I told her it was an emergency. Lynette was brought from her lesson and sounded understandably alarmed. There cannot be many pupils at Benenden whose fathers ring them from pokey motels down in Manly. She feared the worst.

'Daddy?'

'Hello, sweetheart.'

'What's happened?'

'I missed you, that's all.'

'Oh!' A gasp of pure relief. 'Where are you?'

'Australia.'

'Did you win?'

'We don't play until tomorrow.'

'Best of luck!'

'Thanks. I love you.'

'Same here.'

'Sorry about the Dog and Doublet.'

'It was purgatory, wasn't it?'

'How is your mother?' I asked tentatively then added,

146

'How are you, that's the main thing?'

'I'm fine.'

'Good. Just wanted to hear your voice.'

'Take care, Daddy.'

'And you.'

'Come back soon.'

I was too full of emotion to do more than mumble a few words and put the receiver down. My daughter still loved me and wanted me. The trip to Manly had not been a complete waste of time. There was some future to my past.

Having paid for the call, I summoned a taxi and took the long overland route back. Memory had had its fling. It was time to address more pressing matters. I was to be the crucial figure in a transaction between Warren Oxley and the kidnappers. It was a daunting task that was fraught with ugly possibilities and it was only the hope of rescuing Diane Reinhold that reconciled me to it. Her safety was my primary concern.

Before that, however, there was the Skins Game and I tried to focus all my attention on the event. I would be pitted against three supreme golfers on a supremely difficult course. Coping with Gil Jericho would be my major problem. If I let his antics disrupt me, I would be beaten before the start. I had to block him out. During my last practice round at Greenblades, I'd come to terms with many of its hazards. My morale was high. With a combination of skill, pertinacity and boldness I could yet come out on top. It would be a pleasure to relieve Oxley of such a sizeable amount of money.

I got back to my hotel in confident mood. For the first time since the kidnap, I actually looked forward to playing golf. When I went into my room, however, the situation altered dramatically. I sensed at once that something was wrong and soon saw what it was.

My golf bag was missing. It had been stolen.

A victory by Alan Saxon was no longer on the cards. Someone had made sure of that.

CHAPTER FIVE

THE HOTEL MANAGEMENT RESPONDED PROMPTLY. Their chief security officer was sent up to get full details of the theft and to shower me with apologies. As a personal guest of Warren Oxley, I was a VIP and was treated accordingly. The officer was a big, muscular Turk with the kind of face you would not like to meet on a dark night in Istanbul. He had already set things in motion.

'All staff are being questioned,' he said. 'One of them may have seen something.'

'What if the clubs are still in the building?'

'I considered that, sir. A thorough search has been organised. Every nook and cranny of the hotel.'

'You can't search six hundred odd rooms.'

'That will have to wait until tomorrow when the staff go in to change the beds. What I can guarantee is this: if your bag is still on the premises, it won't get out during the night.' He sighed. 'My guess is that we're far too late.'

'Why do you think that?'

'They are professionals, sir. That door was not forced. They were in and out of the hotel in a flash.'

'Somebody must have noticed them carrying a golf bag across the foyer,' I said. 'It can't exactly be a regular occurrence at midnight.'

'In Turkey we have a proverb, sir – "He who steals a

minaret knows where to hide it." If you take something distinctive, you find a way to conceal it. Your clubs may have gone out disguised as something else. And they would certainly have used the fire exit.'

As soon as he went off to supervise the search, the police arrived and I told the story all over again. It was nearly one o'clock when I rang the call-me-at-any-time number that Jan Cummings had given me. She spoke over her bedside phone and was quite obviously alone. That pleased me a lot. She was as shocked by the news as the hotel management and cracked into action fast. I was given another display of the power of Warren Oxley's name.

At seven-thirty, Vic dropped me off outside the largest golf shop in Sydney which had been opened in my honour by the owner himself. He had a vast range of clubs and conducted me around them with pride. Choosing the make was the only easy part of the exercise. My own clubs are custom made, based on a computer analysis of my clubhead speed, my swing path and the position of the club face at impact. All my idiosyncrasies are met. There was no chance that a set of standard clubs would do that.

I picked out thirty or more. Selecting those with a loft and lie that best suited me, I took them around to the golfing range and put them to the test. I must have hit well over two hundred balls before I whittled them down to a bare thirteen. They were far from ideal but they were the best I was likely to get in the situation. The final club to be chosen was the most important of all – the putter. Clive Phelps once did a breakdown of my game over a whole season. The putter accounted for an amazing forty-four per cent of shots, almost half of any round.

Woods claimed twenty-five per cent and some thirteen per cent was taken up by wedge shots. My iron shots were very much the also-rans. Clive pointed out that I only used my 9-iron once in the whole season. And I muffed the shot.

Mindful of all this, I hovered over the putters with the sort of ghoulish fascination I bring to completing my VAT return. The decision has to be arithmetically perfect in both cases or heavy fines can ensue. Also, of course, the two are interdependent. The wrong putter can leave some very nasty marks in my Account Book.

There was a small artificial putting surface in the shop and I spent an age tapping balls towards a metal hole that pinged every time I hit the jackpot. It was the sort of exercise that could have been quite amusing on a rainy day during a holiday. Hours before I was due to play in a major golf event, it was scarifying.

I got it down to three but none was reassuring. It was my own fault. I belong to the Faithful Old Putter school of thought and have hung on through thick and thin to the magic implement that took me to my British Open title at Carnoustie. It's been repaired time and again but its age is a comfort to me. We grew up together and I could never discard such an old friend. Some golfers seem to change their putters as often as they change their socks as if newness is a recommendation in itself. Others again have a high breakage rate when they are let down by their trusty weapon on the greens. I've never struck a blow in anger at my putter, taking the commonsense view that it is only as good as the hands in which it is held.

How I missed it now! I felt amputated.

When the choice was finally made, I loaded my new bag into the Mercedes and told Vic to drive me to the course. The one consolation was that the first round did not begin until after lunch. I could have the rest of the morning trying to get acquainted with my fourteen new clubs, though, in truth, a year would not have been long enough. Frank Davey was waiting for me. Summing up the situation at a glance, he took a positive attitude.

'Limit the number you use,' he said.

'I intend to, Frank.'

'Driver, 3-wood, 5-iron, pitching wedge. They'll get you round most of Greenblades.'

'It's the putter I'm worried about.'

'Give it a whirl.'

'I'd love to meet the man who stole my bag!'

He grinned. 'Love to meet him after you met him.'

We got to work. By eliminating some clubs altogether, I was able to concentrate on the crucial handful and develop a feel for them. Frank's navigation was brilliant. I was only once forced to take a long-iron out though I had more practice with the sand wedge than I wanted. The putter improved slightly at each hole but it had nothing like the swingweight and reliability of my own. It was a respectable round but it did nothing to stave off fears of the inevitable.

I was fatally handicapped.

One of the others would definitely win.

Publicity for the big event had been effective and sustained. Thousands of spectators descended on Greenblades to see what was billed as a sort of unofficial world championship of golf. It was a ludicrous claim but quite in keeping with Warren Oxley's style. He himself was in fine form. Dressed in a white suit and a Panama hat, he was a study in affluence, a smug, smiling and avuncular creature who revelled in the bustling scene. Watching his bearded composure, it was hard to believe that his wife was being held hostage, that his Australian champion was forced out of the contest and that the British representative had his clubs stolen the previous night. Warren Oxley was calm and benign. He fielded media questions with political smoothness.

'Is your wife not here today, Mr Oxley?'

'No, my friend. She's indisposed.'

'Nothing serious, I trust?'

'A gastric infection. The doctor advised rest.'

'But she's a fanatical golfer, isn't she?'

'That's why the decision was such a hard one on her,' said the caring husband. 'Diane will have to watch it all on televison. She's in the best place.' He beamed at the camera to send her a message. 'Take care, darling. We'll do our best to give you a feast of golf.'

Oxley knew how to hog the limelight. Instead of fading into the background so that battle could commence, he insisted on introducing each one of us individually. Herm Wexler was first, wearing a red shirt and tartan trousers. He squinted nervously in the glare of the afternoon sun and looked anything but a world-class golfer. Sam Limsong came next, tall, cadaverous and dressed in blue, forever raising his straw trilby with excessive politeness. I was the third in line and got the biggest response yet from the crowd, who mixed grudging cheers with good-humoured barracking. Australian galleries are nothing if not very involved and very vocal.

Top of the bill, inevitably, was Gil Jericho, the man in black, the hot favourite who was going to vindicate the reputation of Australian golf. He played to the crowd in his usual way but he was not as cocky as I expected. When I first discovered the theft of my clubs, the name of Gil Jericho had gone straight into the list of suspects. It was not something he would do himself but I did not put it past him to organise the raid. He would know just the sort of friends who would do it. In the event, however, Gil seemed genuinely upset by my bad luck and did not gloat over me at all. I put this reaction down to deviousness and kept him pencilled in among the possibles.

As we adjourned to the first tee, it was apparent that this was no ordinary Skins Game. Oxley had blown it up into an international incident. Herm was the arrogant Yank with the get-out-of-my-way swagger (poor casting). Sam was the inscrutable Oriental who had become a one-man version of the Yellow Peril. I was the Whinging Pommie with a supercilious attitude to my colonial hosts. And Gil was the local Action Man, ready to put the rest of us to flight with a firework display.

We were not golfers. We were gladiators.

I wished that I at least had my own trident.

'On the tee, Herman Wexler ...'

It was easy to tell us apart. Our caddies wore the national flag T-shirts to denote our country. Besides, we were supposed to embody all that was worst in our nation. With the exception of Gil Jericho, that is.

'On the tee, Sam Limsong ...'

Wexler's drive had found the green, albeit at the very back. The courteous Thai lifted his hat to the gallery before teeing up his ball. He was not flattered by the company. Over the last few years, he'd become the leading player in the far east, supplanting Tanizaki by virtue of superior range and consistency. Two seasons on the US circuit had transformed him. Critics might complain about the hat routine and the cleverbugger grin beneath it but he was now an exceptional golfer.

'On the tee, Alan Saxon ...'

The support was warm and drowned out the jeerers. As I glanced around, I saw that Jan Cummings was applauding fiercely. It was a tiny comfort but I was grateful for it. Wexler and Limsong had both played controlled drives into a strong headwind. I hoped I could do the same. I went into my ritual, tried to forget that I'd never used the 3-wood in competition before, adjusted my grip to reduce power, then hit the ball exactly where Diane Reinhold would have advised. The sweat on my forehead dried instantly.

'On the tee, Gil Jericho ...'

He did not let his fans down. My swing is merely stylish but his was spectacular. He wound himself up like a spring, held the pose for a second, then uncoiled with venomous force to produce the flashiest shot so far. The gallery loved it and with good cause. It was ten yards closer to the flag than any of us.

We strolled purposefully down the fairway. Most of the spectators followed us but others preferred to watch our progress on the television screens in the hospitality tents. Warren Oxley was ferried along after us in a buggy that bore his name in large letters. He might hate golf but he was interested in seeing where his money went.

A Skins Game is not for the faint-hearted. It's for the gambler with strong nerves. Each hole has a price on it. The first six holes at Greenblades were fifteen thousand dollars each, the next six were worth twenty thousand each, and the last six went up to twenty-five thousand. The normal accumulator system applied. If a hole was halved, the money available on the next hole was doubled. And so on. It's a cut-throat form of golf but I love its exhilaration. You play shots in a Skins Game that you'd never attempt in a tournament. Unlike strokeplay, it does not demand a high standard of golf over four patient rounds. It's simply a question of hitting the right shot at the right time. You may struggle for most of the time then one hot hole can win you a small fortune.

Gil Jericho opened his account at the first hole by

tapping in for a birdie. Only Herm Wexler got his par. Sam Limsong and I three-putted to the amusement of the watching multitude. The next three holes were tied. When we reached the fifth – a 397-yard par four – it was Australia's turn to shine again. Jericho produced a shot that was worth every cent of the sixty thousand dollars that it earned, a stupendous 8-iron approach that rolled to within a foot of the pin. It looked as if he was going to beat us with talent alone. No hint of any gamesmanship so far. As we followed the strutting black figure to the sixth tee, we felt a twinge of poverty.

Sam Limsong remedied the situation slightly. A monstrous forty-yard putt over a rolling green helped him to birdie the hole and collect the prize money. The hat came on and off several times. It was Herm Wexler's big moment on the seventh, a short hole with a tricky left-to-right slope on the green. Encouraged by a smile from the loyal Mary Anne, he hit a 5-iron that set the gallery alight by bouncing off the flagstick to assure him of a certain birdie. Had he achieved a hole-in-one, he would have won a fifty thousand dollar bonus as well, a high price to put on his wife's smile

Two tied holes got us to the turn and I was still well out of the money. My clubs inhibited me. The others were taking more risks and playing better shots. Our next target was the shortest hole on the course, the 131-yard tenth that was set on the headland and exposed to the full bite of the wind. The tee shot had to be played across open water to a circular green that was about thirty yards in diameter. As I'd learned on previous outings, it was embarrassingly easy to overhit the ball and ensure it a burial at sea. Given the conditions, Frank handed me a 6-iron, a club I'd not used before. First time lucky. My tee shot stayed low to defeat the wind, clipped the nearside of the green, bounced off the lip of a bunker and ended up only a yard or so from the hole. Sam Limsong lost his ball overboard and raised his hat in farewell. Herm Wexler barely clung to the perimeter of the green. Gil Jericho ruined a fine tee shot with a weak putt. I birdied the hole to take my first dip into the kitty.

Sixty thousand dollars for that 6-iron.

Jericho fell in beside me to give his opinion.

'That was a fluke.'

'Thanks for the seal of approval.'

'You're playing rubbish.'

'I know – I'm playing you.'

'They're right about Alan Saxon. You're a has-been.'

'I always was.'

'Stop boring everybody with shit golf.'

The words were spoken out of the side of his mouth so that nobody else heard them. They were as puzzling as they were annoying. He must have known that such snide comments would make me fight even harder. Not that my redoubled efforts paid off. The consecutive par fives were tied, leaving Jericho to collect seventy-five thousand dollars on the par four thirteenth with a magnificent approach shot to the green out of heavy rough. The fourteenth fell to America and the fifteenth to Thailand. I felt that I owed it to Diane to excel at the sixteenth hole since it held so much significance for us. Having negotiated the dog-leg carefully to set up a 5-iron approach, I found my worst bunker yet and lost all hope of success. Herm Wexler was the victor. I took solace from the fact that Jericho's tee shot went into the trees down the left and my only regret was that Sheba was not there to retrieve it for her master's collection.

The Australian had another dig at me on the quiet but it did not inspire me to higher achievements. I played the last two holes well but came up against the limitations of my putter. With my own clubs, I might have been a rich man. Gil Jericho won the seventeenth and the last hole was tied. There'd been some sensational golf to dazzle the spectators and the dominance of their player sent them off to celebrate in style.

Warren Oxley stepped back in front of the television cameras again to shake us all by the hand and wish us luck for the second round. His bonhomie was disturbing. Did he really care so little about the predicament of his wife? Surely some emotion should show through? I was still jangled by Rosemary's kidnap and we were not even married any more. What sort of a man was Oxley?

The festivities broke up and we trudged off to the clubhouse. Frank was silent beside me.

'Penny for your thoughts,' I said.

'Forty grand.'

'Can't afford it, Frank.'

'Tomorrow. First hole. Forty grand.'

'Fifty more for a hole-in-one.'

He whistled. 'Ninety grand for one bloody shot!'

'Gives us something to dream about.'

But we both knew it would never happen. Even with my own clubs. With my new ones, I'd be lucky to pick up a hole or two. Frank was on a percentage of my winnings and I felt I was letting him down.

'Can you get here by eight tomorrow?'

'Seven.'

'Why not? I need all the practice I can get.'

'Give 'em hell.'

'Think I can?'

'There for the taking.'

'Gil is the front-runner.'

'One snag.'

'What's that?'

'He doesn't want to win.'

When the Press conference was over, I had a quick drink in the crowded clubhouse then slipped away quietly. I'm not gregarious and never comfortable in a room with more than half a dozen people in it. Besides, I had much to think about and there was no chance of rational thought amid the braying golf talk in that smoky atmosphere. I would not be missed.

Vic opened the door for me and I got into the front passenger seat. The Mercedes purred away. I decided that it was time to exploit an under-used resource.

'Mr Oxley was in good form this afternoon.'

'Was he?'

'Calm, relaxed and full of the joys. You'd never think his wife had been snatched by kidnappers.'

'Mind if we talk about something else?'

'Sore point?'

'Very.'

I gave him a few minutes then tried again.

'Did you ever drive Beverly Nashe?'

'All the time.'

'What was she like?'

'Okay.'

'I'm told she could be a bit of a handful.'

'Could she?'

'Beverly wanted to have her own way.'

'Who doesn't?'

'Did she really burn down that yacht?'

'What yacht?'

Vic was stonewalling me. I bowled a googly.

'What make is that gun you carry?'

'How did you …'

'Colt? Beretta? Mauser?'

'No.'

'Smith and Wesson?' His discomfort was all the

confirmation I needed. 'You wouldn't have it unless you were ready to use it. Ever shot anybody?'

'What's it to you?'

'Curiosity. Come on. Ever fire it?'

'Once or twice.'

'On target?'

'I only carry it for safety.'

'Yours or mine?'

'Hers.'

'Diane? What about Beverly?'

'That was different.'

'Didn't you pack a pistol when you drove her?'

'No need.'

'Why not?'

He clammed up on me and I gave him ten minutes before I resumed my drilling operations. Vic was staring straight ahead through the windscreen and doing his best to pretend that I was not there.

'Who did you tell?'

'Eh?'

'The night you drove me home from Point Piper. I told you I wanted to be at Greenblades by eight the next morning. Who did you contact?'

'Jan Cummings.'

'She fixed it all up?'

'That's her job.'

'So very few people would've known that Diane was going to be on that course with me.'

'Yes.'

'Jan herself. Oxley, of course. The club steward or whoever it was that opened up for us. That's about it.' I turned to him. 'Apart from you, Vic.'

'What d'you mean?'

'You were in on the secret as well.'

'I'm the chauffeur.'

'Chauffers know how to use the phone. You had

some very valuable information in your hands. There must be people who'd pay a lot for it. I met three of them.'

He bristled. 'What are you saying?'

'That you deliberately let us get out of sight at the sixteenth. That you took your time coming to help me. That you did what you were told and collected your loot.'

'It wasn't like that!' he snarled.

'You're in on this, aren't you?'

'Shut up!'

'I think they bought you, Vic.'

The car screeched to a halt and an angry hand pushed me back against the door. I found myself staring down the barrel of a Smith and Wesson ·38. As I looked up into his blazing eyes, I was given my answers.

Yes, he had shot people before. No, he was definitely not involved in the kidnap. I was right on both counts. My accusation had wounded his pride.

'Sorry, Vic. My mistake. You're too loyal.'

'Just you remember it.'

'Put the gun away first.'

'I liked her. I want her back safe.'

'That's something we're agreed on, anyway.'

'So don't push me. Right?'

I nodded enthusiastically. To my intense relief, he let go of me and put the gun back inside his uniform. The car was soon in motion again. I offered an olive branch.

'Tell me about Sydney Harbour Bridge ...'

Hotel security had failed to track down my clubs on the premises. It was now a police matter. They were looking into it. I feared that they would not be looking all that hard. On my personal Richter scale, the loss of

161

my golf bag was registered as a major earthquake: to the police, it was an indiscernible blip. Sydney came up with much greater tremors by the hour. Oxley might lend the weight of his name, but I held out little hope. The city's police force had far more serious crimes to solve.

I entrusted my new clubs to the chief security officer and went up to my room. A long, ruminative soak in the bath took some of the sting out of the day. I rang for sandwiches and coffee. Lounging on the bed in the white bathrobe, I remembered that it had been worn by Jan Cummings a couple of nights earlier. I tingled all over and the waiter wondered why I was grinning when I let him in. When I'd eaten my supper and meditated at length on the mystery of Warren Oxley's second marriage, I recalled that the highlights of the Skins Game were being shown on television.

The set came on by remote control and I changed channels until I found the correct one. We were on the fifth and Gil Jericho was playing his winner to the green. Rapturous applause as he birdied. Jericho raised his club aloft but not with his usual cockiness. By his standards, it was a mild celebration. I watched him at each hole and the same thing happened whenever he got his nose in front of us. Though keen to delight the home crowd, there was an air almost of reluctance. Was Frank right in his assessment? Didn't Jericho want to win?

Why not?

Something else caught my attention. I was totally unaware of it at the time but the replay showed how one man walked inside the ropes held by the stewards and kept only about ten yards behind us. To be more exact, behind me. It was as if he was appointed as my bodyguard and I found it a chilling thought. Was I under threat myself? I would have been less distressed

162

if my minder had not been a man with a centre-parting. Lee Whitfield.

I was watching myself hit that fine tee shot at the sixteenth when the telephone rang. Killing the sound, I picked up the receiver and heard a weary voice.

'Saxon?'

'Is that you, Clive?'

'What's left of me.' He sounded in pain. 'I'm ringing from the casualty department at the hospital.'

'Why?'

'Popped in for a hernia transplant!' he sneered. 'Why do you think I'm ringing from here, you clunkhead? I'm fucking well hurt! Thanks to you.'

'I'm on my way.'

'Bring some grapes.'

'How bad is it?'

'They think they can stick one of my legs back on,' he joked, 'but they've written off both my arms.'

'What are you holding the phone with?'

'I'm not a man to boast.'

'Which hospital?'

Clive gave me the details then added a request.

'Bring that envelope.'

'What envelope?'

'The one I gave you, idiot! With those photostats.'

'Any particular reason?'

'You'll see.'

He rang off and I dressed at speed. The last thing I saw when I switched off the television was the face of Lee Whitfield behind my shoulder. He was glancing around. Probably looking to see if there were any more dogs he could shoot.

The taxi got me to the hospital in ten minutes. Clive was sitting on a plastic chair in one of those long corridors that serve as an echo chamber. He looked bad. His face was puffed, his lip swollen, his left eye black. A thick bandage was tied around his head and another bound his right hand. I sat beside him.

'What happened?' I said with concern.

'He hit me first.'

'Who?'

'That's the bit I don't know.'

'Where did it happen?'

'As I was leaving the Press Club.'

'Alone?'

'I was on a promise,' he groaned. 'Switchboard girl at the hotel. Offered to plug me in so that we could have a private chat. I'd had a few but that only makes me walk straighter. Anyway, as I went past this alley, I was yanked into it. Just one of them. A big bastard who could give punching lessons to Mike Tyson. All over in seconds.'

'What do the doctors say?'

'Nothing broken, nothing torn. I can go home. One of the walking wounded.' His good eye hardened. 'The sod who stitched me up had the gall to tell me I was lucky. Lucky! Christ, I was bleeding pints when I got here! If that's luck, I'd hate to see misfortune.'

I calmed him down and consoled him. Clive had gained his injuries in my services. He'd asked wrong questions in wrong places and someone took exception. That could mean only one thing. We had stumbled on to something.

'Jericho and Whitfield are mates,' he said.

'How did they meet?'

'Rattlesnakes always know where to find each other.'

'Are they old friends?'

'Look, I'm not writing a major biography of them,' he sighed. 'I just made a few enquiries. Then I got hauled into the alleyway for a quiet chat.'

'Is Lee Whitfield interested in golf?'

'Even less than Oxley. His sport is fucking.'

'Men or women?'

'Either. Whitfield is ambidextrous. I'm glad I didn't meet him in that dark alley.'

'Eric would've been very jealous.'

'Piss off!'

The expletive was accompanied by a jab from his elbow that he regretted immediately. Clive was throbbing with pain. When a nurse clacked past us, he did not even look up at her. He needed to be taken back to his hotel.

'Did find out one thing, Alan,' he gasped.

'It'll keep.'

'Whitfield is a gambler. Compulsive.'

'Nightclubs?'

'He'll bet on anything. That's where Gil comes in.'

'How?'

'Far as I got. Far as I can go.'

'Thanks, Clive. You did well.'

'As long as you don't tell me I'm lucky!' He put a hand to his head to hold in the pain. 'Where's that envelope?'

'Right here.' I offered it to him.

'Find that photo of Diane Reinhold at college.'

'Why?'

'Just do it.' I took out the photostats and leafed through them. 'I established another connection tonight.'

'Did you?'

'They were at college together.'

'Who?'

'Give me the photo.'

I eventually found it and passed it over. It was taken at the University of Melbourne. Diane Reinhold was addressing an audience from a platform. Sitting behind her at a table were half a dozen students watching her with rapt attention. Clive stabbed a finger at the young woman who sat at the end of the table. Long hair, black hornrims, an expression of academic intensity. Her baggy sweatshirt disguised her figure.

'Don't you recognise her?' said Clive.

'Should I?'

'Look more carefully.'

'Sorry. I don't know her.'

'Take off her glasses. Shorten her hair. Put her into something svelt.' I followed his instructions but was still baffled. 'Imagine it was a colour photo. Think of all those sexy freckles.'

I was jolted. When I scrutinised the girl's face, I saw why Clive was so pleased with his discovery. I also wondered why she herself had not mentioned this link with Diane Reinhold. They were not just fellow-students. They were leading members of some organisation. The girl in the hornrims and the baggy sweatshirt set off my emotional burglar alarm.

It was Jan Cummings.

I felt robbed.

Vic collected me early next morning and ushered me into the rear of the Mercedes. He made it quite clear that my days of sitting beside him were over and that he was not up for even the most neutral conversation. Frank was waiting for me at Greenblades beneath a menacing sky. Dark clouds were scudding in from the sea and the wind was stronger than ever. We were in for a squall.

Like my caddie, I was keen to get down to business and familiarise myself a little more with the new tools of my trade. My insecurity had made my game too cautious on the first day so I tried to be more audacious now. It made for some outrageous errors but it also delivered some welcome surprises. The stakes were high and I just had to gamble everything.

All the stops had to be pulled out. Frank was pleased that I'd used only half the clubs in my bag. Some would simply be there for the ride.

Rain threatened us throughout but it did not fall in earnest until we were on the eighteenth tee. After four well-spent hours, we hurried off to the locker room. I seized the opportunity to clarify something.

'You said something that puzzled me, Frank.'

'Did I?'

'Gil Jericho not wanting to win.'

'That's how it looked to me.'

'In what way?'

'He didn't try hard enough on certain holes.'

'Are you certain?'

'I was until this morning.'

'What do you mean?'

He nodded towards the course. 'When I got here at six-thirty, he was just starting his round. Keen enough now. He certainly wants to win today.'

'And will he?'

'Doubt it.'

'Why?'

'Gil hates rain.'

We had a light meal together in the clubhouse and talked about the second round. Times have changed. In the old days, professional golfers would never have socialised in this way with their caddies. The distinction between masters and men was scrupulously observed. Caddies were knowledgeable local men who might run a plumbing business or work as park keepers when they were not lugging a bag around a golf course. They waited until the tournaments came to them and kept their hand in at weekends with club members. In our own more enlightened times, the full-time caddie is in the ascendant, the bright, talented, ambitious young man who carries a golf bag as a prelude to his own career as a professional and who – if he makes himself indispensable – may travel the world with a player. I know caddies who stay in the best hotels wherever they go and who would turn up their noses at the idea of a night in a motor caravan named Carnoustie. They have high standards and a large income to support them.

Frank was one of the old school who had made the transition to the new. He'd served his apprenticeship as a menial at the golf clubs of Sydney. Now he was one of their top caddies. His Maserati was in the car park.

'What's the state of the betting?' I said.

'Changes at every hole.'

'Australia still favourite?'

'Yeah. Odds shortened to 2-1 on after those first five holes. Limsong was next at 5-1. You and Wexler fell away badly and the word had got round about your clubs.'

'And at the end of the day?'

'Gil Jericho is still way out in front. Rest of you are all 4-1. That's not a bad bet.'

'On me? Or on them?'

He smirked. 'Wait and see.'

The storm had really settled in now and play was delayed by half an hour until the driving rain eased off into a drizzle. Conditions were very unpleasant and I noticed how tense Gil Jericho was. Weather such as this could make a nonsense of any form and he was no longer such a hot tip. The Skins Game was up for grabs.

Warren Oxley introduced us again then sloped off to the clubhouse. He was a fairweather spectator. One man who did brave the elements, however, was Lee Whitfield who trailed us all the way with the stewards. I thought his presence would be inhibiting until I realised that he was no longer keeping me under surveillance. His interest had switched to the home challenge and it was Gil Jericho who was under examination.

Aware of the high price on the first hole, we went for it with all guns blazing, peppering the green with our tee shots and being over-eager with our putters. None of us made par and the hole was tied. Two more tied holes sent the value of the fourth up to seventy thousand dollars and nerves really began to fray as we took on the 590-yard par five. The wind lengthened it even more and we needed three shots to reach the green. Sand knocked me out of contention and Herm Wexler misjudged his first putt to shoot way past the hole. It was Jericho against Limsong with the Thai in the less favourable position. His putt, however, was perfectly weighted and seemed to be directly on line. A slight deviation at the last moment cheated him out of a birdie and a psychological hold. Gil Jericho took far longer than usual to line up his own putt but his care was repaid. Though not the most convincing shot, it did trickle apologetically into the hole.

Australia was off again. The relief shown by Jericho was matched by that on the face of Lee Whitfield. They were playing this round together.

I pinched the fifth with the kind of putt they call a character-builder then Herm Wexler entered the fray to take the sixth and seventh. Gil Jericho claimed the next hole with an imperious eagle that left the rest of us scrambling in his wake. The jauntiness had fully returned to him now and he was shooting out remarks to goad or undermine us. His breezy insolence was not justified. Greenblades would give him nothing more.

It was Sam Limsong who now went on a charge. A bedraggled figure in a sodden hat, he conjured up some real magic to poach the next three holes on the trot. My moment of glory came at the twelfth hole when, with the wind at my back and the adrenalin pumping, I hit a second shot that came within a yard of a double eagle. I slid it into the cup to earn myself another twenty thousand dollars and some caustic asides from Gil Jericho. He was still ahead of us and believed he was impregnable. But he reckoned without the caprice of golf.

Sam Limsong birdied the thirteenth to take another bite out of the prize money then the miracle occurred. At the fourteenth, the last short hole on the course, Limsong used a 2-iron from the tee to hit the shot of a lifetime. Helped by the wind and guided by whatever gods were on duty that day, the ball hit the apron of the green and sped like an arrow towards the pin. When it dropped into the hole, the gallery erupted. The straw hat was not just raised but hurled into the air. Fluke or not, the hole-in-one had relieved Warren Oxley of a cool seventy-five thousand dollars and carved a permanent grin on Sam Limsong. It had also thrown Gil Jericho into a frenzy.

He could now be caught.

'Freaky bastard!' he muttered.

'Great shot,' I said.

'Never do that again in a million years.'

'He doesn't need to, Gil.'

'Look at the stupid cunt, will you?'

'Sam's entitled to celebrate.'

'Won't get another fucking chance!'

But the prediction was false. Though Jericho tried everything he knew within the laws – and a few things outside them – he could not capture another hole. It was not because of me. I stuttered badly over the next three holes but Herm Wexler and Sam Limsong were in superlative form, matching the Australian to force a tie each time. Everything now rested on the final hole. The odds were very much in Jericho's favour. Only the beaming Thai could stop him now. If Herm Wexler or I snatched the glittering prize, it would still leave Jericho as the overall winner.

My challenge faded with my second shot, a loose 3-iron that dropped well short of the green. America was the next to drop out with a bad hook into trees. Sam Limsong got closest but he was in a bunker. Gil Jericho was twenty yard adrift of the hole. Herm Wexler did some lumberjacking for his third shot and I chipped on to the green. Gil Jericho now had a golden opportunity to thrill his fans and make his victory emphatic. He crouched over his ball for a long time and the stress took its toll. There was much more than a hundred thousand dollars at stake and he could not handle the pressure. The putt was firm but well off line. He had opened the door.

Sam Limsong went through it with aplomb. Out of wet sand, he played a delicate shot that rolled lazily into the hole and made him the overall winner with a final tally of three hundred thousand dollars.

I was the first to congratulate him and the sporting Herm Wexler was right behind me. Gil Jericho's handshake was an act of contempt before he stalked off.

I stole a glance at Lee Whitfield.

He wanted to shoot more than a dog.

The presentations took place under the cover of an awning and Oxley once again basked in the occasion. Though I had the smallest cheque – ninety-five thousand dollars – I was happy enough. In spite of the conditions, it had been an exciting contest and I did better than expected with a replacement set of clubs. In two rounds of golf at the formidable Greenblades, I'd earned twice as much as in the whole of the previous year. Yet I came last.

We moved off to the locker room to shower and change before joining the crowd in the clubhouse for a general celebration. Clive Phelps was not going to miss out on that. Unlimited free champagne would have fetched him out of his coffin. Making light of his injuries, he got stuck into the buffet with relish. I managed a jostled word.

'Did you follow us around?'

'On the telly in here.'

'Best place, Clive.'

'I saw some amazing things.'

'Gil Jericho working through his repertoire?'

'More amazing than that. Oxley had a visitor.'

'Oh?'

'They went off together for a long time.'

'Who was it?'

'Pass me another glass of that excellent champagne and ask me how I am. I need sympathy.'

I handed him a drink. 'How are you?'

'Sound as if you're interested, damn you!'

'How are you, Clive?' I soothed.

'Bloody awful! These injuries have played havoc with my love life. The doctor told me to take it easy. "What about sex?" I asked. "Be very careful there, Mr Phelps. No excitement at all. Stick to the wife".'

Clive cackled at his own joke but suffered for it.

'Who was the unexpected visitor?'

'Don't rush me.'

'Oxley went off with him, you said.'

'No, I didn't. Because it wasn't a him.'

'A her?'

'Beverly Nashe. In the flesh.'

'Are you sure?'

'Dead sure,' he confirmed. 'My balls were throbbing for an hour afterwards. It was Bev okay. How could any man throw something like that out of bed?'

'Was Oxley surprised to see her?'

'He was delighted. Gave her a tickertape reception then whisked her off somewhere.' Clive slipped an arm around my shoulders. 'Alan, old son, I do wish I had even the faintest idea of what's going on. Have you?'

'Ask me tomorrow.'

Sam Limsong came up to give me a courteous embrace then Clive nabbed him for an impromptu interview. I went across to spend a few minutes with the Wexlers, who were over a hundred thousand dollars richer than when they arrived. They are always pleasant company and I was annoyed to be detached from them by Jan Cummings.

'The car is waiting outside for you,' she said.

'But I'm not ready to leave yet.'

'Mr Oxley wants you now.'

'Let him come and find me then.'

'You have to deliver something.'

My objections vanished and I followed her out. Diane Reinhold needed me. Vic was at the wheel of the Mercedes. Lee Whitfield held the rear door open for me then got in beside me. As we drove away, a limousine followed us. Warren Oxley and another man were in the back. I could sense Vic's nervousness. His body was tense and he was driving with extreme care. I put it down to Whitfield's presence. He was enough to unsettle anyone.

I turned to look into his smouldering eyes.

'Where are we going?'

'Never mind.'

'I'd like to know.'

'Shut your mouth.'

'What's the deal?'

'I won't tell you again.'

Silence fell and nobody broke it for well over an hour. Vic took us along what was evidently a rehearsed route. We were in open countryside when he pulled the car over and gingerly applied the handbrake. The other vehicle stopped behind us but nobody got out.

'What are we waiting for?' I asked.

'Darkness.'

'Why?'

'They're calling the shots.'

'The kidnappers?'

He said nothing and his glare discouraged me from trying to strike up a conversation. We sat there for about half an hour while the shadows lengthened outside. Lee Whitfield had an educated menace about him. I could just see him presiding at a board meeting, making harsh decisions with brutal unconcern, justifying the ways of Warren Oxley to ordinary men. He was a whizzkid in a six hundred dollar suit, a hoodlum with a degree in Business Management. I've had more amenable companions in the backs of cars.

The wait unnerved Vic who began to tap on the steering wheel with his fingers. Whitfield stopped him with a click of the tongue then glanced at his watch.

'Drive on,' he said. 'Carefully.'

The Mercedes took us on for another ten miles or so until we came to a fork in the road. Vic brought the car to a gentle halt and wheezed slightly. The other car stopped a hundred yards behind us. Leaving the keys in the ignition, Vic got out and walked back in the darkness. Whitfield motioned me to get out. I obeyed.

'Are we here?' I said.

'Not quite. You go on alone.'

'Why?'

'Instructions.'

'Can't Vic come with me?'

'Just you.' He lifted the boot. 'And this.'

I looked at the small suitcase and guessed what it contained. Whitfield handed it to me and closed the boot. He indicated that I should get into the driver's seat and put the case beside me. Then he gave me a dark smile.

'Up to you now, Saxon.'

'What do I do?'

'Take the left fork. Drive for five miles and stop. Don't go above thirty. That's most important. You'll find yourself in the middle of a plain. Wait there until they come and find you. With Diane.'

'Then?'

'Make the exchange.'

'And?'

'Get her out of there fast.'

He closed the door and watched through the window as I checked the controls. Compared to Carnoustie, it was like being in the cockpit of an aeroplane. Dials told me everything I needed to know and several things I did not. I gunned the engine, put the car into forward drive and let the automatic gearbox take over. It was wonderful. We glided along at thirty-five with no sense of effort or noise. It was more like floating than driving.

The other vehicle did not follow. I was alone with a million dollars and a pounding heart. The closer I got to my unknown destination, the more I began to speculate on what could go wrong. The kidnappers might just grab the suitcase and hang on to Diane. They might already have killed her and be waiting to finish me off as well. I was alone, unarmed and inexperienced at this kind of thing. I was being sent naked into the conference chamber.

After five miles, I stopped the car and switched off the ignition. I was on flat open ground but the darkness prevented me from seeing more than a few yards of it. I waited for ten minutes with the sweat starting to pour. Nobody came. Another ten minutes had my mouth dry and my teeth chattering. Still nothing. To divert myself, I reached for the suitcase and flicked open the catches. I'd never seen a million dollars in neat bundles before and I took some of them out to flick through them. It was a gruesome moment. The thick wads were fakes. They had real money on the top but slips of paper underneath.

With mounting anxiety, I checked the other bundles and learned the worst. They were all fakes. There was probably no more than a few thousand dollars in the suitcase and I was about to hand it over to someone who would count it with meticulous care. They would not be amused. Warren Oxley had set me up.

I was a human sacrifice.

My first instinct was to turn the car around and drive straight back to confront them but I was too late. Distant lights flashed three times in my rear view mirror. It was a signal to another vehicle that was up ahead of me. With its full beam on, it began to move slowly towards me and I had to shield my eyes with my arm. Stopping fifty yards away, it dipped its headlights and allowed me to make out the vague profile of a van. It was probably the one used in the kidnap though there were no ladders on the roof rack.

I lowered my window and waited. Someone shouted a command from the van. The voice was deep and rough.

'Get out with the money!'

I did as I was told. Caught in the glare of their headlights, I was lonely, fearful and unprotected.

'Put the suitcase on the bonnet!' I did so. 'Walk towards us with your hands in the air.'

'Let me see Diane first.'

'Do as I say!'

'Not until I know that she's safe.'

There was a pause then a massive figure got out of

the van and stood on the edge of the light. We'd met before. He liked chloroform. Another man got out and motioned someone forward with a gun. As she stepped into the light, I saw that it was Diane. She was wearing a balaclava like the two men but I recognised the clothes she'd been wearing at Greenblades. It looked as if the kidnappers were ready to fulfil their side of the deal. What would they do when they learned that Oxley was not?

'Hands up. Walk forward!'

I followed orders and walked thirty yards or so.

'Stop there!'

Leaving Diane by the van, the two men loped towards me. While the one held a gun on me, the giant searched me with unceremonious hands. He grunted his verdict.

'He's clean.'

As he went off towards the car, I glanced over my shoulder. Several things flashed through my mind. Vic's nervousness. Lee Whitfield's presence in the car. The steady way it was driven. The speed limit imposed on me. The suitcase with the fake ransom. It all added up.

The Mercedes was a booby trap.

Even as I lurched away from it, the car exploded with a suddenness that lit up the sky for miles around. I was knocked to my feet with the force of the blast but at least I had my back to the explosion. My companion came off far worse and was completely dazed by the impact. He screamed in pain as he rolled on the ground. The Mercedes was a ball of fire. Somewhere in the middle of it was the huge man and a charred suitcase.

Shaken but only bruised, I got to my feet and raced across to Diane, pushing her into the passenger seat of the van then running around to get in beside her. I felt for the ignition key but had no chance to turn it on. A gun was held against my ear. With her free hand, the woman pulled off her balaclava and glared at me.

It was not Diane Reinhold.

My travel arrangements deteriorated. Instead of sailing along in the luxury of a Mercedes, I lay tied up in the rear of the van, sliding helplessly to and fro whenever we went around a bend. They had not bothered to clear the vehicle out. It was stocked with rolls of cable and a selection of television aerials. A couple of power drills lay out of my reach in a wooden box. The man and the woman in the cab were having an animated conversation as they drove along but I could not really hear it. They kept mentioning a name that sounded like Des. I took him to be their late colleague. Des would not be able to give me the chloroform treatment again but I might well be in for a far worse fate.

We bumped along over an uneven surface for a while then joined what felt like a proper road. The speed now increased and we held it for the best part of half an hour. I estimated that we were at least thirty miles from our rendezvous. Without warning, we swung sharply to the left and I was hurled against the side of the van. Our pace was slower now and we were going up a hill. The engine was labouring and the driver changed down. When we halted with a jolt, I was all but spiked by antennae.

Doors slammed and the back of the van opened. The man grabbed me and hauled me angrily out. When I fell to the ground, he kicked me to get up. I was dragged into a small building and pushed up some stairs. There was a light on the landing and I was able to see that my captors were both wearing balaclavas. I turned to enter a plea for the defence.

'That bomb was nothing to do with me.'

'Keep moving.'

'I was supposed to die as well.'

'You will.'

They pulled back two bolts, twisted a key in a lock then thrust me violently into a room. It was gloomy and unwelcoming but it contained the two things I most wanted to see at that point in time – Diane Reinhold and my golf bag. Both apparently unharmed.

Diane was sleeping on the floor under an old blanket and stirred as we burst in. She was bound hand and foot and wearing her underclothes.

'Alan! What are you doing here?'

'Just happened to be passing.'

The woman pushed me aside and confronted Diane.

'Your fucking husband tried to blow us up!' she yelled. 'He'll pay for that – the bastard! If he wants his precious wife back, he can have her. In bits.'

When Diane tried to speak, the woman slapped her hard across the face. The man moved in with a piece of rope to tie my feet together. He gave me another kick to relieve his anger then went out. The woman paused to sneer at us.

'Enjoy your last night together!'

She slammed the door and we could hear the key being turned and the bolts being shot home. Footsteps went off down the stairs. My immediate concern was for Diane.

'How are you?' I asked.

'Could be worse.'

'How have they treated you?'

'Not too badly.'

She struggled to sit up and the blanket fell away to reveal bare shoulders and midriff. Her hair was ruffled and her face and body were bruised. My anxiety deepened.

'They didn't …?'

179

'No, Alan. Nothing like that, thank God. The big one talked about it, especially when he'd been drinking, but she kept him in line. She's the boss.'

'Who are they?'

'I wish I knew.'

'How many?'

'Four.'

'Three,' I corrected. 'The big one is dead.'

I told her what had happened and how I came to be part of it all. Diane listened with horror and shook her head in disbelief.

'Warren wouldn't do a thing like that.'

'Yes, he would.'

'I know him. He'd pay the ransom.'

'With a car bomb.'

'Warren would put my safety first.'

'Then he's slipped up somewhere along the line.'

We were interrupted by the sound of a car in the distance. It approached with speed and skidded to a halt. The front door of the house was opened. I rolled over a few times and used the wall to lever myself up into a sitting position. Raised voices came up the stairs. The kidnappers were having a fierce row and the woman's authority was not prevailing. Feet pounded up the steps and our door was unlocked. A sturdy man in shirt, denims and balaclava charged into the room, lifted me up against the wall and started to pummel me with both fists. I was grateful when the woman and the other man raced in to restrain him. My attacker cursed them and tried to shrug them off but they held fast.

'I'll kill him!' he howled at me.

'What are you like in a fair fight?' I gasped.

'Des was my mate!'

He lunged at me again but they clung to him and somehow managed to calm him down. When they felt able to release him, his attention turned to Diane. He stood her against the wall and pulled out a long knife.

'We'll give your husband till noon,' he said with the point at her throat. 'This time Oxley delivers the money himself. Otherwise ...' He slipped the blade under the front of her bra and cut through it to make her breasts spill out. 'I come back and cut off your tits.'

He meant it. He glared at me to show that I would be included in his carving programme then slouched out. The others followed him and the door was secured once more.

Still reeling from all the blows, I slithered back down into a sitting position and averted my eyes from Diane who was vainly trying to cover her embarrassment. We heard a door open downstairs and voices raised in farewell. A minute later the car drew away and roared off. At least one of them had gone. We could not afford to be there when he came back. I cudgelled my brain for a means of escape.

Diane tried to put a brave face on it all.

'Who won the Skins Game?'

'Sam Limsong.'

'I would've backed you.'

'No chance without my favourite caddie.'

'You must wish we'd never played that round.'

'It had its moments.' I glanced at the door. 'Think they'll come back up again?'

'Probably not. I've been alone most of the time.'

'What about visits to the bathroom?'

'You hang on until breakfast. About seven.'

It gave us room for manoeuvre. I glanced around for something that might sever our bonds but the room was empty. To break the window would make too much noise. There had to be another way but it was proving elusive. Aching from my punishment, I looked around the room again until my eye fell on my clubs. It was wonderful to be reunited with them. I fantasised about how I would have played Greenblades with them at my disposal. Frank was just handing me my putter for another birdie opportunity when a thought hit me like a sledgehammer.

Golf could be our salvation. The game which got us into the trouble could also get us out. Among the many odd things I carry in my golf bag is a penknife. It might take a long time to cut through stout hemp but it was better than nothing. The bag stood close to Diane. I lay on the floor and rolled across to her.

'Where are you going?' she said.

'Ease the bag against me.'

'What?'

'It'll make less noise that way. Come on.'

'Why?'

'Just do it.'

Diane nudged the bag towards me and I took its full weight so that I could lower it gently to the floor. With my hands tied behind my back, it was not easy to open the zip but I eventually managed it. After scrabbling around among the golf balls and tee pegs, my fingers closed on the penknife. Opening it was a trial of patience. Every time I thought I was winning, the blade snapped shut, twice cutting my finger and drawing blood. When the penknife twisted out of my fingers, Diane moved across.

'Let me try. My nails are longer.'

'Open the small blade. It's easier.'

'So I noticed.'

She had her setbacks as well but her pertinacity got her there in the end. The blade flicked open. I backed up to her in the half-dark and felt the warmth of her body. We held hands in silence and drew solace from each other. Then I took the knife from her and tried to saw through the rope around her wrists. It was slow, painstaking work but it gave us the chance to talk.

'Where did you meet Warren?' I said.

'Alice Springs.'

'How did that come about?'

'He asked me to lunch.' A quiet laugh. 'I'd been working in the outback on my research into Aboriginal Songlines. I'd got drawn into their way of life. They almost accepted me. Then a mining company planned to excavate on land that was an ancient burial site. The Aboriginals couldn't take on the might of capitalism. They asked me to help and do you know what I found?'

'The mining company was owned by Warren.'

'Yes,' she said. 'I always believe in going to the man at the top so I drove into Alice and rang him. I got through to him and tried to put my case. He made me an offer. Have lunch with him and he'd listen.'

'All on the strength of a phone call?'

'Not quite, Alan. I discovered later that he knew who I was. Saw an article about me in a magazine. Dreadful piece entitled "The Nun of the Outback".'

'Enough to fetch any man running.'

'Warren came in his private plane. Lunch lasted for about twenty-four hours. Yes, I knew he was married at the time but that was already breaking up. I had no guilt on that score.' She shrugged. 'I liked him, it was as simple as that. Convinced that I'd hate the man, I found that we somehow got on. That's how it started.'

'And the mining operations?'

'He cancelled them.'

'You were the heroine of the hour.'

'Only for a while. As soon as we were married, he instructed the company to go ahead and drill. Their lawyers soon saw off any objections. All I'd done was to delay the inevitable.'

I paused to rest my fingers. The effort of hacking away at her ropes and my nerves were telling on me.

Sweat was running from my armpits. I thought of what lay ahead if we did not escape and began to saw away more vigorously. Diane pushed back harder against me.

'You think I sold out, don't you?' she said.

'Not up to me.'

'It's what everyone else thought. That it was a kind of betrayal. I was turning away from everything I'd ever believed in. Not true, Alan. I married Warren for the freedom to do my own thing. I didn't change.'

'What about Warren's reputation?'

'It terrified me. Until I saw it was an illusion.'

'Carefully fostered by your husband himself.'

'Oh, yes. That's part of his charm.' She winced as I jabbed her wrist by mistake. 'Warren is not perfect. He can be arrogant, cruel, uncaring and as male chauvinist as they come. But he has a good side to him as well and that's what he shows me. I love him.'

I believed her but it was not the point at issue.

Did Warren Oxley love her?

Another pause, another burst of energy and we were almost there. As the strands of rope began to part, I put all my strength into my filing action and it worked. I cut through. She pulled off the rope and rubbed wrists that were red and raw. Then she turned quickly around to attend to my bonds. She untied my hands then we loosened the ropes around our respective legs. I then removed my Pringle sweater and offered it to Diane. Pulling it on, she kissed me on the lips in gratitude. I got a second kiss when I produced a pair of waterproof trousers from the recesses of my golf bag. They were much too big and had to be rolled up but they made her feel dressed.

'Do you know where we are?' I said.

'Miles from anywhere.'

'What have they told you?'

'Nothing.'

184

'What's out here?' I said, crossing to the window and straining my eyes against the darkness.

'A sheer drop. No way out.'

'Not even with these ropes?'

'Much too steep. The door is the only exit.'

I tried turning the handle and applying force. The door did not budge. If that was our exit then someone would have to open it for us. With one person, we might stand a chance, especially if it was the woman. But if there were two of them downstairs, both armed, then we would not be able to overpower them. Cutting off the ropes had only given us a small measure of liberty. We were still trapped.

A faint rumbling came to my ears. It grew and grew in a steady crescendo. The sound took me to the window where I saw two distant lights piercing the blackness like laser beams. The roar came nearer all the time. A monster was abroad.

'What's that?' I said.

'A road train.'

'Sounds enormous.'

'It is. Watch.'

We stood at the window together. Far below us, the lights slowly altered course and curved away from us. Sidelights enabled me to pick out a gigantic lorry that was powering its way along with two equally gigantic trailers attached to it. The gross tonnage must have been staggering but that was not my main interest.

'What's down there, Diane?'

'Just that road.'

'Distance?'

'About three hundred yards away.'

'How many vehicles go past?'

'The occasional road train is all I've heard.'

'Then that's our way out.'

'Is it?'

'We simply attract the attention of the next one.'

'How, Alan?'

'Wave the blanket or something.'

'They wouldn't see it,' she argued. 'We're too high up here. Besides, if they did spot a blanket flapping out of a window, they wouldn't take a blind bit of notice. These are Aussie truckers, not Good Samaritans. They've got schedules to meet so they'll pass by on the other side. We'll get no help from that quarter.'

'We must, Diane. It's our only hope.'

'What about Warren?'

'Forget him.'

'But he'll have men out looking for me.'

'They haven't found you so far.'

'He'll pay the ransom this time.'

'Not a chance.'

'Of course, he will,' she argued. 'I'm his wife. He'll do anything to get me back. Warren will come in person to hand over the money.'

'He can't, Diane.'

'Why not?'

'Because he knows it would be suicide. They're not after the money any more. They want him. He's not going to walk into a trap like that. Let's face it. They'll come back empty-handed.'

Cold terror made her shiver all over and I took her in my arms to comfort her. We hugged each other tight.

'Alan ...'

'Yes?'

'Get us out of here. Please.'

CHAPTER SIX

DAWN CAME EARLY TO DRAW back the curtain and reveal a bleak landscape. A plain stretched out towards the horizon with nothing to break it up except an outcrop of rock or a few trees and bushes. The road that snaked its way below us for mile after mile was covered in dust. A stream meandered nearby without conviction. The house itself was virtually derelict. Perched on the top of a hill, it could only be reached by a rough track that corkscrewed its way up. As light flooded into our room, I saw that the walls were peeling and the floorboards starting to rot. Insects were beginning their day.

The window opened out on to a balcony that was in dire need of repair. Part of the wooden balustrade was broken off to give an uninterrupted view of a sheer drop of some fifty yards or more. The kidnappers had chosen the place with care. Our room was a prison cell.

I was standing on the balcony and gazing around in desperation when I noticed the dot in the far distance. Diane came at once in response to my signal. We watched the dot get slowly bigger until we could hear its rasp. It was a high-powered motorbike, tearing along and leaving a cloud of dust in its wake. Two helmeted figures were crouched low over the machine as it slashed its way through the silence. I grabbed the blanket and waved it in the air like a flag but they paid no heed. Shooting around the bend in the road below us, the motorbike accelerated away with disdain. It had somewhere to get to and no compassion to spare.

'It's hopeless,' said Diane.

'Pray for another road train.'

'How can we make that stop?'

'I'm working on it.'

I went back into the room to ponder further. As I groped around madly for a solution, I caught sight of my golf bag lying on the floor. A wild notion took root. I went back out to the balcony and stood near the gap on the balustrade. There was no wind and the rising sun was brightening up the target every second. I mimed a practice swing with my arms.

Diane came across to me in consternation. Doubt and fear showed in her face. I forced a smile.

'Can you think of a better idea?'

'No,' she admitted.

'I'll need a caddie.'

She nodded and went into the room to take my driver from the bag. When she unzipped the pouch, she took out the three balls and held them in her hand.

'Is this all we have, Alan?'

'One good shot will do it.'

'But there's hardly any margin for error.'

'That's golf.'

I wrapped the blanket around the broken edge of the balustrade to deaden the sound then I snapped some more struts off. The gap was much wider. I took the driver from her and had a few tentative swings. There was just enough room for me. Handing the club back to her, I went to fetch my penknife and some tees. By gouging a hole in the balcony, I was able to insert a tee and ram it in tight. We experimented with a ball. It sat up nicely on the tee. My name glistened in the sunlight.

Using the penknife again, I inserted two more tees in line with the first and six inches apart. If and when the chance came, there'd be no time for leisurely preparation. All three balls would need to be dispatched in about thirty seconds. A passing vehicle would not wait until I had gone through my usual routine. I nodded to Diane who set the other two balls on their respective tees.

She looked up at me with scepticism.

'This isn't going to work, is it?'

'Probably not.'

'What do we do then?'

'Improvise.'

She gave me a wan smile then scanned the horizon. We did very little else for the next hour or so, watching for the faintest sign of movement, waiting for a vague promise of deliverance, praying for a miracle. The sound of music came from the room below as a transistor was switched on. Feet then came up the stairs and we froze in horror. Our plan would be discovered and we would be tied up again. Diane came instinctively into my arms and I could feel her heart beating. We braced ourselves for something that never came. The door was shaken then the feet retreated. Our visitor had simply wanted to check that we were still securely locked in.

We were still recovering from the shock when we saw the new dot on the horizon. It was moving more slowly than the motorbike and enlarged steadily to monstrous proportions. Another road train! Heaven had heard us. We were in with a chance.

I pulled the glove on to my left hand and swung the driver a few times. Given the sharp incline, the distance was within my compass and I would have been confident of reaching a green from there but my task was much more complex. I had to hit a moving target through a narrow window of time. A ball that bounced off one of the trailers would be wasted. The lorry was the bullseye.

The vehicle thundered on with callous unconcern. It wanted to ignore us completely and surge past. Our plight was a hindrance. I had to persuade it otherwise. Within the next minute, I had to play the most important shot of my life. If I failed, it would undoubtedly be my last.

'Good luck!' whispered Diane.

'We'll need it.'

I studied the juggernaut carefully to estimate its speed then I addressed the nearest ball, drew back my club and let fly. My first drive was a range-finder. It fell short of the road, bounced on across it and landed up in the stream. Now for the ones that counted. I waited until the road train was close enough, then I unleashed a drive with full power, recovering at once to send the third ball rocketing off while its predecessor was still airborne.

The first ball veered to the left and clipped the last of the trailers before bouncing harmlessly away, but the second had a more fortuitous flight. Hit hard at a different angle, it came down just short of the road, took a deflection from a boulder and shot straight through the windscreen of the cab. The road train went into a series of convulsions and zigzagged violently before halting in a small dust storm a hundred yards down the road.

Diane hugged me in congratulation, but our troubles were not over yet. I'd stopped the vehicle but the two men inside were far from pleased. When they jumped out of the cab, one of them was brandishing a tyre lever. They saw us waving from the balcony and ran towards the rough track that led up to the house. These were no knights in shining armour coming to rescue us. They were brawny truckers who were yelling with rage.

The commotion was noted in the room below us and a shot rang out, sending the two men diving behind a rock. At the same time, footsteps charged up the steps and rushed us off the balcony. As the bolts were flung back, I stood behind the door with the driver in my hand. Diane backed off into a corner. The door swung open and the man came in with his gun at the ready. My downward swish of the club cracked his wrist and knocked the weapon to the floor. Howling with anger, he turned to grapple with me and tried to wrest the driver from my hand. Diane had the presence of mind to kick the gun clear of us. As she bent to pick it up, however, the man found the strength to hurl me bodily at her. The two of us fell in a heap and he closed in to recover his weapon. I lashed out with my own foot and sent it sliding out to the balcony and over the edge.

The man flung himself on me in a fury and got a grip on my neck but Diane came to my aid. Grabbing my club, she swung it hard at the man. He put up an arm to parry the blow and gave me the chance to roll him off. Both of us got to our feet. Shots from below told us that the two truckers were still trying to move forward. Diane raised the club again but the man grabbed it, snatched it from her grasp and hit her with a punch. I tackled him low and brought him crashing down. Hurt by the blows from the club and winded by the fall, he yet had enough energy to get me in a neck hold and drag me slowly towards the balcony. Fear gave me extra impetus and I jabbed him viciously in the stomach with my elbow, twisting out of his relaxed grip and getting a hold of my own.

We were out on the balcony now, risking both our lives on the crumbling timber, grappling and pushing and punching. Eventually, he got my back to the balustrade and put all his effort into one final shove but I was ready for him. Moving quickly to the side, I helped him on his way and his forward thrust did the rest. Screaming at the top of his voice, he smashed through the balustrade and went headlong through the air until he hit the rocks below. As I stood there panting and looked down at the prone figure, Diane came back to my side.

A new danger threatened. Having seen her colleague flashing past her window, the woman came running up the stairs to take revenge. I got to the door first and slammed it in her face but she fired twice through the timber. Both shots sent splinters into my face. When I heard the gun click, I knew she was out of ammunition and opened the door to drag her into the room. She swung the gun at me but I grabbed her wrist and twisted hard until she dropped the weapon. Diane grabbed it. The woman fought like a demon, scratching, biting and kicking for all she was worth. It was all I could do to subdue her. When she brought a knee up into my groin, I lost my temper and swung a punch that knocked her off her feet. She fell heavily and banged her head on the floor before lapsing into unconsciousness.

While I leaned against the wall to recover, Diane bent down to whisk the balaclava off the woman's head. I'd seen the plain, oval face before with its close-set eyes beneath a large forehead. Short brown hair, no make-up, late twenties. What was interesting was Diane's reaction. She swallowed hard and stepped back a pace.

'Do you know her?' I said.

'No.'

'You seemed to recognise her.'

'Never seen her before in my life.'

Before I could pursue the subject, a rifle was fired

outside and a bullet shattered the window of our room. I ran to peer out and saw that one of the truckers was now armed. Evidently, he'd been back to the vehicle to get the weapon and enjoyed using it. Two more shots rang out.

I put my driver back into my bag, slung it over my shoulder and took Diane by the hand. It was time to get out of there fast. The truckers were in no mood to listen to rational explanations. A golf ball had smashed their windscreen and they'd been fired at. Vengeance was the only thing on their mind.

We ran downstairs, out through the front door and across to the van. Hurling my clubs into the back, I jumped into the driving seat and was relieved to see the key in the ignition. I switched on at once.

Diane was still holding the gun she'd picked up.

'What do I do with this?'

'Give it to me.'

'It's not loaded.'

'They don't know that.'

I drove the van wildly down the track until I saw the two men, then I poked the gun out of the window. They dived for cover. We were past them in a flash. A few shots pursued us but we were soon out of range. I headed in the direction from which the road train had come. The truckers had no hope of catching us now. They'd served their purpose in diverting one of our captors. The men would investigate the house then contact the police on their two-way radio. We were well out of it.

Diane laughed nervously with relief.

'You were marvellous, Alan.'

'Don't ever ask me to play a shot like that again.'

'It was superb.'

'Two parts genius, one part fluke.'

The van rattled along at sixty with nobody else in

sight. In any other circumstances, I could've relished being alone with Diane Reinhold. Adversity brought us closer. Now that I knew her better, I saw that she was not a bit like Rosemary. It was refreshing.

My mind went back to the woman at the house.

'Who was she, Diane? You know her, don't you?'

'I … thought I did. It was a mistake.'

'Who did you think she was?'

'It doesn't matter.'

'I happen to think it does.'

'Back off, Alan. Please.'

'Why are you lying to me?' I pressed.

'I'm not lying.'

'What are you hiding?'

'Leave me alone!' she exclaimed then buried her face in her hands. After a few moments, she recovered her composure and sat up. 'I'm sorry.'

'My fault.'

'Still in a state of shock, I'm afraid.'

'Understandable. You must've gone through hell.'

'Ten times over.'

'All the more reason to find out about the people who put you there. Know what my theory is, Diane?'

'What?'

'They weren't holding you to ransom at all.'

'Of course they were.'

'The asking price was too low.'

'What?'

'One million dollars for the wife of Warren Oxley? That's chicken feed! He'd shell out ten times that much without losing a wink of sleep. Warren knew they'd cheat on their side of the deal. That's why I was sent along with that car bomb.' I glanced across at her. 'Everything they did was to get at him. When he set up a prestigious event at Greenblades, they first bumped Rod Melville out of the action then kidnapped you.

When neither actually stopped the Skins Game, they caused further disruption by stealing my clubs. There's a pattern here, Diane.'

'I don't find it very convincing.'

'There're a few bits missing yet.'

'Such as?'

'How Beverly Nashe is involved.'

'Beverly?'

'And where Gil Jericho fits in. I mean, I can't really see him getting along with our friends back at that house. They *believed* in something.'

'What are you talking about, Alan?'

'Politics. That's what this is all about.'

'Is it?'

I shot her a quizzical look but she ignored it. Diane was holding out on me. I decided to try to jolt the information out of her.

'It's time to see Warren as the shit he is.'

'Don't say that!'

'He tried to kill me, Diane. I was meant to go up in smoke with that Mercedes. Explain that away. He knew what the kidnappers would do. Take it out on you.'

'No!'

'Indirectly, Warren tried to kill you as well.'

'That's a terrible thing to say!'

'Not from where I stand.'

'Just because you hate Warren.'

'You ever been thirty yards from a car bomb?'

'I don't believe he'd do any of this.'

'Still think he's a plaster saint?'

'I know my husband.'

'Maybe. But you don't know the one that belonged to Beverly Nashe. He was a different man, by all accounts. He wears the face suitable to the occasion. And to the wife. You're married to a chameleon, Diane. Or you were. Warren wants you right out of the way now.'

'Why?'

I turned to look at her and spat out my opinion.

'Another woman. Jan Cummings.'

She hit me across the face with as much force as she could muster then stared through the windscreen. The next fifteen miles were eerily silent. The more I reflected on it all, however, the more persuaded I became that I was right. Diane was holding out on me. She had information that would confirm much of what I'd said but she refused to divulge it. Love is its own protection. She simply could not reconcile the horrors of what had happened with an apparently doting husband. When she was finally compelled to accept the truth about him, it would be quite devastating. I wanted to be around at the time to help her. Meanwhile, I had another cheek.

The bare landscape had shaded into signs of richer vegetation. A river appeared over to our left then a small forest. As we drove past the trees, we saw a wooden building up ahead of us, a rather dilapidated place with a single petrol pump outside it and a few signs that we could not yet read. Ramshackle as it was, it lifted morale. We had reached civilisation again.

It was still relatively early and the old man in the sleeveless vest did not like being hauled out of bed on a Sunday. He puckered an already wrinkled face.

'Garage is closed.'

'We don't want petrol,' I said.

'Then why wake me up with that bloody horn?'

'This is an emergency,' said Diane.

She launched into an explanation that was clearly baffling the old man so I chose a shortcut and thrust money at him. He brightened at once and even got his wife up to make tea for us. He also let us use his telephone. I was at Diane's elbow as she got through to the house at Point Piper. She winced when the voice of

Jan Cummings answered and flicked me a look of anger.

'Jan? This is Diane.'

'Thank goodness! Are you all right?'

'Just about. Where's Warren?'

'He's out supervising the search for you. They've got helicopters out and everything.'

'What are you doing at the house?'

'Holding the fort. But where are you?'

'About fifty miles north-west of Sydney. That's what the old man says, anyway. He runs this garage. We arrived a couple of minutes ago.'

'We?'

'Alan Saxon is with me.'

'That's great! Hold on a tick while I get a pen ...'

Diane licked her lips. She was very unsettled.

'I'm back,' said Jan. 'Now give me exact details of your whereabouts and I'll pass them on to the command helicopter. Okay? Let's have it.'

The old man had to be pressed into service to help and the details were relayed to Jan. I could only hear her voice faintly but she sounded quite perky. That could not be said of Diane. She was getting irritable.

'Leave it to me,' said Jan. 'Just stay right where you are and we'll get to you. It won't be long. They'll be on their way in no time at all.'

'Thanks.'

Diane put the receiver down and scowled. I withdrew tactfully and chatted to the old man. His wife's tea was an ideal restorative for jangled nerves. Two cups of it had me feeling almost human. Diane slowly revived as well and accepted the old woman's offer of a skirt. After fifteen minutes in the bathroom, Diane came back looking much better but she still studiously avoided my gaze.

We were on another pot of tea when we heard the

whirr of the helicopter. Running out of the garage, we saw it scything its way across the bright blue sky. We waved excitedly and cheered as it began to swoop down towards us. All of Diane's doubts were swept away. Her husband was coming to rescue her and reassure her of his love. When she was in his arms again, she would be safe. She ran forward and semaphored with both arms. I was abandoned and forgotten. A fragment of her past.

My own feelings about the helicopter were mixed. If it contained Warren Oxley, then he would get no tearful thanks from me. I'd want to ask him about who serviced his Mercedes. The helicopter had almost reached us now and I saw that the side door was open. When a figure leaned out of it on a harness, I needed only one glimpse of the sub-machine gun. Darting forward, I knocked Diane to the ground and lay on top of her. Bullets dug a small trench all around us then the helicopter was past and turning for a second sweep. I jumped up, hauled Diane with me, then pulled her towards the cover of the nearby trees. She was almost hysterical as another burst of bullets followed us into the foliage.

'It's me, Warren!' she whimpered.

'He knows that, Diane.'

'What's going on?'

'Follow me.'

I pulled her into the densest part of the forest as the helicopter hovered over us and tried to pick us out. The sub-machine gun's stutter was heard again and the bullets rained down. Through the latticework of leaves, I got my first sight of the man who was firing at us. Leaning out of the helicopter like a commando, he handled his weapon with expertise. It was Vic.

The noise was now deafening and the swish of the rotor blades sent a gust of cold wind through the trees.

We shivered together then scurried to a new hiding place and awaited a fresh attack. It never came. After dipping down to brush its wheels against the topmost branches, the helicopter suddenly rose into the sky and flew off. As one ear-shattering sound receded, another took its place. Two police cars were speeding towards the garage with their sirens howling. The old man ran out to greet them.

Diane looked up at me and fainted in my arms.

Uniformed officers sprinted through the trees.

For the first time in my life, I was actually glad to see a policeman.

A short rest and a fresh cup of tea helped Diane to recover and she was able to corroborate the story that I was telling to such sceptical ears. The police had come in response to a call from the truckers back at the house and had been looking for the van. Their arrival was very fortuitous. It frightened off the helicopter and enabled them to focus on a series of related crimes – the theft of the van, the kidnap, the murder of the giant Des, the shooting incident at the house and the latest attack from the air. I pleaded guilty to causing wilful damage with a golf ball and explained how my assailant had fallen to his death. Diane backed me to the hilt.

Calls were made to Sydney and facts were checked. We were to be driven back by courtesy of the New South Wales Police. I made sure they took my golf bag out of the van then asked for some brief time alone with Diane. There were some things she had omitted from her statement and I wanted to see if I could get them out of her. The senior officer lit a cigarette and exhaled thoughtfully.

'Five minutes, Mr Saxon.'

'That's all I ask.'

'Get moving.'

I took her into a living room and sat her down. We had no time for niceties. I plunged straight in.

'Who was she?'

'Alan ...'

'I deserve to know. Stop holding out on me.'

'Let the police handle it.'

'Don't shrug me off like that,' I insisted, taking her hands in mine. 'My life has been on the line just as much as yours. I'd like to understand why, Diane. Is that being unreasonable?'

'No.'

'Right. Here's the story so far. Stop me if I get it wrong. University of Melbourne. You were a high-flier in the Sociology Department and your special interest was Aboriginal culture. Along with Jan Cummings, you got involved with the environmentalists and that brought Warren Oxley to your notice.' I paused. 'How am I doing?'

'I'm still listening.'

'Your people hated Oxley. He was Public Enemy Number One to them. Yet you decide to marry him. Why, Diane? Was it because he swept you off your feet?' I pulled her to me. 'Or was there a deeper reason?'

A full minute passed before she spoke.

'Her name is Karen Palmer.'

'Who is she?'

'An activist I met at a conference some years ago. I was one of the main speakers.' She looked up at me. 'Do you know much about Greens?'

'Only the eighteen I make my living on.'

'The Green Movement is the most important political development since the war. It's worldwide and knows no barriers of class, creed or colour. It's peaceful, wholesome and getting stronger all the time.'

'But it has its share of psychopaths.'

She nodded sadly. 'You get militants in any group. Karen Palmer was one of them. The Dark Greens weren't dark enough for her and the eco-feminists were too tame. Karen went off to form a splinter group with some other extremists. Self-styled guerrillas on the lunatic fringe of the Green Movement.'

'With your husband on their hit list.'

'He was an obvious target.'

'But well-defended. So they went for you instead.'

'That's how it looks.'

'Did you help them, Diane?'

She recoiled as if from a blow and let out a gasp of pain. Her eyes filmed over but not from the shock. They were tears of remorse. She was suddenly ashamed.

Our five minutes alone had been very revealing.

Police stations are the same the world over. They are much nicer to walk out of than to go into. I didn't even spare the place a glance when we arrived in Sydney. After a high-speed journey next to the somnolent Diane, I just wanted to be somewhere quiet on my own. Instead, we were taken along a corridor and shown into an office that smelled in equal parts of polish, cigarette smoke and human misery. A uniformed policeman stayed with us. Diane remained morose. The events of the last twelve hours had forced her to re-evaluate her marriage and her whole life. I knew something of what she was going through.

The telephone rang and the policeman answered it. He received an order then conducted Diane out of the room. I was left alone with all the old fears stirring. I felt as if I was in custody. My father would like that. I half-expected him to walk through the door to resume his tyranny over me. A long wait finally came to an end and the same policeman returned. He showed Warren Oxley in then wisely withdrew.

I was out of my chair and pulsing with rage.

'Why did you try to kill me?' I demanded. 'Why did you put that bomb in the Mercedes? Why did you send that helicopter to shoot us down?'

He stayed calm and offered me a slip of paper.

'Go on. Take it.'

'You're a complete bastard, Oxley. I'm going to kick seven barrels of shit out of you if you don't tell the truth. I want an explanation.'

'This is it, Alan.'

'Eh?'

'It's a bank receipt. Look at it.'

'Why?'

'Because it proves that I took out a million dollars in cash last Friday.' He thrust the paper under my nose. 'The money was put into a suitcase. My instructions were that you should hand it over to the kidnappers.'

'It was half-full of blank paper.'

'The suitcase was switched.'

'Lee Whitfield!'

'He thought he'd destroy the evidence when that car blew up. But you lived to tell the tale. When he heard where you and Diane were, he made sure his helicopter would be the first to arrive. Then he could have another go at eliminating you. Since you'd obviously told Diane all about it, she had to be wiped out as well. And she might have been – but for you. I'm very, very grateful.'

'Where is he?' I snarled.

'Forget Lee. The police are hunting him right now. So are some men of my own. For his sake, I hope the police get to him first. My men won't take prisoners.'

'I want him. He's mine.'

'Stay out of this, Alan. You've done more than enough as it is. Diane has been telling me. We both owe you a great deal.'

I was baulked. Warren Oxley had deflected my anger and left me flailing. He was not as innocent as he was now pretending, nor would his marriage come out of it all unscathed. I resented the note of condescension in his voice. He was at once thanking me and putting me down.

'Do you know who the kidnappers were?' I said.

'We will do very soon.'

'Why?'

'The police have arrested the two who were still alive.' He gave me a grim smile. 'The others were put out of commission. By you.'

'That leaves Whitfield.'

'Let the professionals handle him.'

'I will,' I promised. 'Afterwards.'

Pushing past him, I ran out of the room and along the corridor. Lee Whitfield was not the only man on my wanted list. There was Vic as well. I had no idea where they might be but I knew someone who might help me.

When he opened the door, I kicked it hard against him and went into the room. He stumbled back and hit the wall.

'Jesus Christ!' he gasped. 'What was that for?'

'Openers.'

'Have you gone crazy, Alan?'

'You ain't seen nothing yet.'

I closed the door behind me and pushed him in the chest. Gil Jericho tripped and fell down on to the bed. He was up again at once, frothing with indignation.

'Keep your fucking hands off me!'

'Try stopping me.'

'What have I done to you?'

'What haven't you done, you prick?'

'Get out!'

'Not till we've had a chat.'

He faced up to me. 'If you don't piss off right now, I'll ring security and have you thrown out on your good-for-nothing Pommie arse!'

He reached for the telephone but I got there first and yanked it hard so that the cable snapped. He rounded on me in alarm.

'You're spaced out, mate! What are you on?'

'It's called anger.'

'Why pick on me?'

'Because you're first.'

'I'm just about to check out.'

He made a sudden dash for the door but I was on him at once, dragging him back into the room and hurling him to the floor. Gil Jericho was no fighter. He won his battles by more cunning means. As he tried to get up, I jabbed a foot and sent him sprawling again.

'Steady on!' he yelled.

'That was for Clive.'

'What the fuck are you on about?'

'That little deal you had with Lee Whitfield.'

'You've lost me, mate.'

'Then let me remind you,' I said, circling him as if about to attack him again. 'You and Whitfield thought you could clean up at the Skins Game. And I was supposed to do my share to help.'

'You're out of your skull!'

'That's why you were so upset when I had my clubs stolen. My chances were very slim. But you stuck to the plan to see if it would still work. Go hell for leather over the first four or five holes to shorten the odds against yourself even more.'

'I'm not listening to any more of this!'

'You've got no choice, Gil.' I hauled him up and pinned him against the wall. 'I've wanted to do this to you for years. You're a disgrace to the game of golf!'

'I beat you, didn't I?'

'Only when your betting coup failed. That was the plan, wasn't it? You and Whitfield spread a lot of money around on Alan Saxon. When you got off to that flying start, they were offering 8-1 on me. That's when your mate put even more on. If I had come through to win, the pair of you would have made a fortune. But I blew it.'

'You were rubbish.'

'So you told me out on the course, Gil. That's when I realised something was up. You were goading me on because so much was at stake.'

'I always say that kind of thing.'

'Not to Herm. Not to Sam. You worked on them in a different way. The sly word, the dirty trick. You tried to slow them down so that I could get up a head of steam. But it just wasn't my day.' I released him and stood over him. 'You and Whitfield must have had a lot to talk about after that first round. When Clive Phelps came snooping around, you weren't in a mood to humour him.'

'I never touched Clive!'

'No, you haven't got the balls for it. Someone else did it for you. I've come back to even the score.'

'Calm down a minute, will you?'

'Only if you shut up!' Another push subdued him. 'Where was I? Ah yes – Day One. Disaster. I let the two of you down badly. Day Two. A rescue bid. Lay out even money on Gil Jericho to recoup your losses and share whatever you could lift from Warren Oxley's wallet.'

'You can't prove any of this, Alan.'

'I won't need to with your confession.'

'Bollocks!'

'I'll have those as well if I have to.' I fixed him with a glare. 'Day Two. Another disaster. When you really tried to win, you couldn't. Even with all that so-called gamesmanship. Sam Limsong played his heart out.'

'Yellow-bellied turd!'

'You always did respect your fellow-golfers.'

'Fuck off!'

'That's the difference between us and you, Gil. We've got self-respect. Every time we step on a course, we do our damnedest to win. We'd never bet on someone else and let him edge us out. It's unsporting.'

'Unsporting!' he said contemptuously. 'Grow up, Alan. Golf's not a sport. It's a machine for making money and you do it any way you choose.'

'You chose wrong both times,' I reminded. 'All that money laid out on me. All that extra money laid out on you. Even with your winnings, you and Whitfield must've caught one hell of a cold.'

'It was his idea!'

'And you were an innocent bystander, I suppose.'

'Anyway, it wasn't quite like you said.'

'Near enough to make no difference.'

'There's nothing illegal in having a bet.'

'You pollute the game. Do you know that?'

He smirked. 'I add a bit of colour, that's all.'

'There's more to it than that this time.'

'What are you on about?'

'Stolen money, Gil. One million dollars.'

His jaw dropped. 'How could you …?'

'Oh, I know lots of things. I know that Whitfield did a switch with the suitcase so that he could get back some of the money he'd lost at the bookies. And since I was the one who let him down at Greenblades, he arranged for me to go off with a bang.'

'That was nothing to do with me, Alan.'

'For once, I believe you,' I said softly. 'Now, in exchange, you can do two things for me. Okay?'

'What are they?' he grunted.

'First – who beat Clive up?'

'I don't know.'

'You're lying again.'

'Lee fixed it.'

'Who did he get?'

'He didn't tell —'

'Who did he get!' I shouted.

There was a long pause before the name squeezed out.

'Vic.'

He did a lot more than drive a car and count rivets.

'Second question, Gil …'

'Go on.'

'The suitcase.'

'Lee took care of that as well.'

'He drove off with me in the Mercedes. That means the switch must have taken place at Greenblades. With an accomplice.'

He glanced around furtively then caught me in the solar plexus with a sneak punch, thrusting me aside and making for the door. I dived after him, caught a leg and brought him down. Gil Jericho was not going to surrender easily. He swung his fists and feet at me as we rolled on the floor but he had nothing like my frenzy to sustain him. I sat across his chest to hold him down and got my hands on his windpipe. His eyes enlarged with terror. I relaxed my grip slightly.

'Where's the suitcase?'

He struggled again until I tightened my grip. Then he shook his head to show that he had had enough. I removed my hands so that he could gasp for breath.

'Where is it, Gil?'

'Still at Greenblades.'

The taxi broke every speed limit and quite a few local records on the trip to the country club. I urged him on and gave him a handsome tip when we screeched to a halt in the car park. Sunday had brought out the golfers in profusion and the course was dotted with action. I ran straight into the locker room where a few more members were getting ready for their weekend round. At the far end of the room, lurking beside a locker, was Vic. He was surreptitiously working at the lock with a small screwdriver and trying to force it.

I walked over to him and held up the key.

'Try this, Vic.'

'Where d'you come from?'

'Gil Jericho.'

'Very convenient,' said a voice behind me.

It was Lee Whitfield, emerging from the doorway to the showers with a gun in his hand. He took the key from me, opened the locker door and pulled out the suitcase. It was identical to the one I delivered to the kidnappers.

Whitfield had a keen sense of symmetry.

'You carry it, Alan. Just like before.'

'Any car bombs this time?'

'Let's go and find out.'

He kept the gun in my back as we headed for the door. The members looked up in alarm and backed away quickly. We went out to the car park and headed for a maroon Rover. Before we could reach it, however, two police cars came tearing down the drive. Lee Whitfield had sharp reflexes. Pushing me to the ground, he grabbed the suitcase and sprinted to the car. Vic jumped into the driving seat and started the engine. As the police closed in, Whitfield fired a couple of shots to slow them down. A tyre was hit on the first car and the second collided with it.

With the exit now blocked, the Rover charged off towards the course itself, scattering members right and left, skidding and sliding on the moist turf. I got up and sprinted madly after them. They were going much too fast to avoid all hazards. They crested a rise on the third hole and nose-dived into a cavernous bunker. I could hear the engine revving and see the plume of sand being thrown up into the air.

The police were in pursuit as well. We ran through an avenue of baying members. A car churning up their beloved fairways! It was sacrilege. When I came panting up towards the Rover, Vic and Whitfield abandoned all hope of getting it going again and clambered out. Vic had obviously been injured in the accident because blood was pouring from his forehead. He was limping badly and I had no trouble in overhauling him and buffeting him to the ground. One punch was all I could spare him. It made him groggy and left him there until the police came.

My quarry was up ahead, cutting across the green towards a clump of trees, holding the gun in one hand and the suitcase in the other. The memory of what he did to me put more air in my lungs and fresh power in my legs. Lengthening my stride, I began to gain steadily on him and got loud encouragement from the onlookers. Aware of me behind him, Lee Whitfield turned to fire a shot as he ran but it went well over my head.

He was into the trees now, charging through the undergrowth but slowing all the time. The suitcase was a hindrance that kept catching on trunks and bushes. When I got within yards of him, he turned again to shoot and my left shoulder came on fire. It only put extra urgency into me and I made one supreme effort. As he slowed to go around some bushes, I flung myself headlong after him and tackled him around the ankles.

Lee Whitfield came crashing down and the gun was knocked from his grasp. He swung the suitcase at me and tried to get up but I was not leaving go now. Hurling myself on top of him, I held his head in both hands and banged it against the ground time and again until he was begging for mercy. When the police dragged me off, I was ready to pass out.

Clive Phelps was waiting for me at the hospital. He was ogling the nurses as I walked slowly towards him. A welcoming grin lifted the bushy moustache.

'Here he is – Lazarus!'

'Don't joke about it.'

'Risen from the dead.'

'Half-risen.'

'Alan Saxon. The biggest comeback since condoms.'

'You might ask how I am,' I bleated.

Clive beamed. 'I might – but I don't think I'll bother just now.' He inspected the bandaging around my left shoulder. 'Sewn it back on again, have they?'

'The bullet grazed my shoulder. Nasty flesh wound.'

'Serves you right for having nasty flesh.'

'They wanted to keep me in for a night but I insisted on being discharged.'

'I just did the same but she wouldn't play ball.'

'Take me back to my hotel, Clive.'

'Hey, I'm injured, too!'

'We'll take each other back then.'

'You're on, old son! Then I want the full story.'

'Exclusive to you.'

'The Aussie Press are going to love that! Talking of which, I don't suppose you caught today's papers?'

'Too busy writing tomorrow's headlines.'

'The Dastardly Digger has been repulsed.'

'What?'

'Agnew and Pollock. They won't be buying up Millward Latimer. The takeover bid was fought off. Harvey Jansen is *virgo intacta*. Our publishing careers have been saved by a whim of Fate. We won't have to write our books for Warren Oxley, after all.'

'Best news I've had all week.'

'Wait till you see the barmaid at the Regent,' he said with relish. 'Tits? Biggest pair in the southern hemisphere. I bet they've got a larger collection of fingerprints than Scotland Yard.' He grinned amiably. 'Like me to put in a word for you?'

'Another time, Clive.'

'You've got no sense of adventure.'

'It's Sunday.'

After a couple of hours and a lot of drinks, Clive left me alone in my room. I opened the window to dispel the cigar smoke. My head ached, my shoulder hurt, my whole body was crying out for tender loving care and attention. Before I could take it off for resuscitation in the whirlpool bath, I was halted by the ring of the telephone.

'Hello?'

'Alan?'

'Diane!' I said in surprise. 'How are you?'

'Fine.'

'You don't sound it.'

'I've been checked out by the doctor. He says I stood up to the ordeal remarkably well. What I need now is plenty of rest.'

'Don't we all?'

'But how are you?' she said with concern. 'I heard about the trouble at Greenblades.'

'Jinx course for me, one way and another.'

'They told me you were shot.'

'Flesh wound in the shoulder. I won't be playing any more golf this year, I'm afraid. Have to miss out on the South Australian Open next week. Pity. I love Adelaide.'

'It's all my fault,' she said quietly.

'Don't be silly, Diane!'

'It was my bright idea to stage the Skins Game.'

'You weren't to know that we'd end up trying to save our own skins. Besides, it's all over now. Water under the Sydney Harbour Bridge.'

'I'm sorry, Alan.'

'No apology necessary.'

An awkward pause. 'I've done a lot of hard thinking since I got back. It's been very painful. I'll be going away tomorrow for a long holiday.'

'Alone?'

'Warren doesn't figure in my plans for the future,' she said bluntly. 'That phase of my life is over.'

'How does he feel about that?'

'He'll soon find someone else.'

'Jan Cummings?'

'You were wrong about her, Alan. There was nothing going on between them. She's not even employed by Warren any more. He sacked her this afternoon.'

'Why?'

'Ask him.' Another uncomfortable pause. 'I'm not very good at saying thank you, Alan.'

'Then skip it.'

'But you did so much for me.'

'I always spoil my caddies.'

'More to the point, you made me think. That's why I feel so dreadfully guilty now. It was what you said to me back at that garage.'

'I said a lot of things.'

'You asked me a rather brutal question.'

'I remember. Did you help them?'

'I was stunned at first. And insulted. But not any more. You see, I did help them. Without realising it, I gave them all the assistance they needed. Goodbye.'

The line went dead. I was mystified. Though pleased that she was breaking away from her husband, I could not fathom her last remark. I stifled the impulse to ring her back for clarification. Diane Reinhold had brought me nothing but danger. Her place was now in my past. There was some recompense for all our suffering. Warren Oxley had had a calamitous week. He'd lost his wife, his right-hand man, his chauffeur. He'd also lose some credibility. At a time when he most wanted to project a good image, he would be deluged with bad publicity. There was another bonus. After the chaos of Greenblades, he would never want to go near another tournament. He and Gil Jericho would now be permanently exiled from the world of golf.

I'd done sterling service to the game.

A light tapping on my door disturbed my reverie.

'Who is it?' I called.

'Jan.'

She was the last caller I'd expected and I felt the swirl of mixed emotions. Anger, regret and affection were tempered by curiosity and I moved swiftly to open the door. Jan Cummings was wearing a stylish red dress of patterned silk. A red scarf was tied roguishly around her neck. She looked at once vivacious and penitent.

'Hello,' she said.

'Hi.'

'How's the shoulder?'

'Still attached to the rest of me.'

'Can I come in, please?'

'Sure.'

'There's something I want to say.'

I stood back so that she could walk past me then I closed the door and followed her in. When I indicated a chair, she shook her head. I lowered myself on to the sofa and waited for her to speak.

'You're a brave man, Alan.'

'To let you in here again?'

A wry smile. 'That, too, I suppose. But I was thinking about Diane. You saved her life.'

'I know. She's leaving her husband.'

Jan strode away from me a few paces. I was reminded just how beautiful her long legs were and wondered if that was the object of the exercise. She turned to me.

'You must be rather puzzled by it all.'

'Totally bewildered.'

'That's why I came. To try to explain.'

'I wish somebody would, Jan.'

She took a deep breath. 'Diane and I first met at university. We were in different faculties but we both belonged to this environmental group. I was keen but Diane was really dedicated. She ran the thing. We used to send petitions and organise protest marches and try to raise the general consciousness about Green issues. Australia was being polluted in the most systematic and frightening way. By people like Warren Oxley.'

'He hasn't changed.'

'That's the problem. Diane thought he would.'

'What do you mean?'

'I remember her making this speech in which she said that it was no good taking on the big corporations from the outside. They were too well defended. What we had to do was to infiltrate them. Work from the inside.'

'Is that what you were doing, Jan?'

'No,' she admitted. 'I sold out. Once I graduated, I went into the job market. I wanted to be a career girl and enjoy the fruits of success.' A sigh of remorse. 'That's how I drifted into Warren's clutches.'

'And Diane?'

'She stayed true to her principles. Her research kept her in touch with environmental issues. Literally. I mean, you don't spend all that time in the outback unless you're wholly committed. The sacrifices are enormous. It's very primitive.' She shrugged. 'Anyway, Diane got drawn into this dispute over Land Rights. They were going to drill on some Aboriginal Burial Ground.'

'Diane told me. She rang Warren direct.'

'At my suggestion. First off, she contacted me.'

'Oh.'

'Her idea was to send a protest letter but he gets dozens of those a week. The Shit Pile, he calls it. The letters get shredded as soon as they come in. Warren never even gets to see them.'

'What did you advise Diane?'

'To include her CV with the letter to give it more credence – she's highly qualified. I told her to ring him up the next day and I'd make sure she got put through. Meanwhile, I stapled her letter to an article about her. It was a big colour spread from a magazine – the one that Beverly used to edit.'

'The Nun of the Outback.'

'That's it. Fascinating stuff. How she lived with the Abos and spoke their dialects. Turned her back on civilisation. Searched for the true Australia.' She walked towards me. 'Oh, yes. Then there was the golf.'

'In the outback.'

'Diane built her own course,' she said, sitting down beside me. 'Nine holes in some God-forsaken spot in the Northern Territory. She didn't so much design it as take what nature offered her. There was a photo of the course in the article. Diane was teaching some little Abo how to swing this home-made club.'

'How did she get interested in the game?'

'She was born to it.'

'In New Zealand?'

'Her father was the pro at Christchurch Golf Club.'

'I've played it,' I said warmly. 'It's in a garden suburb

called Shirley. Nice course. Toughest hole is the fourth, a tricky par five that runs along the boundary fence.' I smiled. 'Sorry. Let's come back to the letter.'

'I gave it to Warren and he was about to scrunch it up. Then he saw the pictures of Diane. He was still drooling over them when she rang up.'

'So it was lunch in Alice Springs.'

'He believes in whirlwind romances.'

'The problem was that he was still married.'

'Beverly was out of control. She had to go. He didn't dare tell her about Diane.'

'So he found a decoy. You.'

I remembered what Beverly said about finding her husband in a compromising situation with Jan Cummings. It had all been stage managed to get one wife out of the way and make room for the second.

'Did Diane really love him?' I said.

'At first. And she was quite a catch for him. Marriage to her gave him a halo effect. He presented himself as the caring face of capitalism!' She gave a sardonic laugh. 'Nothing could have been further from the truth. Diane found that out when it was too late. She thought she could inculcate her ideas and values but he was only playing along.'

'What about her old chums in the Green Movement?'

'They said she'd betrayed them.'

'Going over to the enemy.'

'Warren wasn't the only target for the extremists after that. They wanted to hit out at Diane as well.'

'So she did help them. Indirectly.'

'Yes, Alan. She was a symbol.'

I thought of Karen Palmer with a gun in her hand. The kidnap was as much about humiliating Diane as about hurting Warren Oxley. They would have got as much money as they could out of him before they let his wife go, then they would have used it to subsidise the propaganda fight against him. Lee Whitfield's intervention changed all that. I didn't play well enough for him at Greenblades.

'What about Beverly Nashe?' I asked.

'Beverly?'

'She turned up at the clubhouse on the second day.'

'Instinct. She sensed that something was up. Diane had gone to such trouble to set up that Skins Game and yet she wasn't there. Warren claimed that she was ill but Beverly saw through that.'

'So she came to enjoy his discomfort.'

'Of course. She smelled blood.' Jan laughed harshly. 'Beverly will have a wonderful gloat when she hears that Diane has moved out. Working for Warren Oxley is going to be like living in a nuclear testing zone. I'm glad that I'm finally out of it.'

'I'm told that he fired you.'

'He owed me one last favour.'

Jan Cummings crossed her legs and looked steadily into my eyes. We were friends again and she was pleased about it. She glanced at my shoulder again then looked up with a questioning smile.

'Do you need a nurse?'

'I'll let you know.'

'How long are you staying?'

'Until the first available flight home.'

'Have we scared you off?'

'I've got urgent business waiting.'

'Who is she?'

'A sexy little number called VAT return.'

Jan Cummings laughed then leaned across to kiss me softly on the lips. A burning sensation in my shoulder helped me to fend off temptation. We got up and went to the door. I opened it and stood back. Jan touched my cheek gently with her hand.

'What will be your chief memory of Australia?'

'Dog biscuits.'

She giggled happily and walked out of my life.

Jan was a bundle of contradictions and I was ready for the simpler pleasures. I was sorry to miss the other tournaments in which I'd agreed to play but at least I would not be handing them over on a plate to Gil Jericho. Sydney was making me restive. Compared to my plush suite at the hotel, Carnoustie was primitive but I missed her companionship. There was no danger of finding Warren Oxley waiting for me in my motor caravan.

Fatigue massaged me all over. I was about to head for the whirlpool bath when the telephone rang again. With a weary sigh, I picked it up and listened. There was a moment of silence then a voice trilled in my ear.

'Daddy?'

'Lynette, darling.'

'You're paying for this call so I'll keep it short.'

'Where are you?'

'At school. We're rehearsing for the play.'

'Marvellous to hear you!'

'I just couldn't wait to tell you the news,' she said. 'That's why I sneaked out of the rehearsal.'

'Well?'

'It's all off!'

'What is?'

'The marriage. Mum and Dreary David.'

'Are you sure?'

'I had a call from her this morning. She finally rumbled him. So she's given him the old heave-ho.'

'I thought you liked David.'

'Only because he kept Mum off my back.'

'What happened?'

'She wouldn't give details. That means one thing.'

'What?'

218

'David failed the Bedroom Test,' she said airily. 'All my friends here warned me that he would. I just don't think he had enough sex drive.'

'Don't be unkind, Lynette.'

'I'm just being realistic. I mean, he was nice enough in his own creepy way but he was never going to be a hunk.' She giggled irreverently. 'What woman would want to lie down on his couch?'

'I'm sure there's a deeper reason, Lynette.'

'Mum didn't go into that.'

'I sympathise with him.'

She chortled. 'Why? He's had a narrow escape.'

It was heart-warming to hear her in such high spirits and I could have talked to her for hours. But a stern voice bellowed her name in the background.

'Must go, Daddy. They want me.'

'See you soon, darling.'

'Great news, isn't it? Just the three of us again.'

'Yes, Lynette. Just the three of us.'

She rang off and left me quite elated. The marriage was off and I'd regained something that I'd learned was very important to me. Rosemary was part of my identity. The thought of losing her had sent me running off to Australia to play golf. I could now return home and welcome her back into my life again. She would be cold, acerbic and critical but I could handle that version of Rosemary. What I could not accommodate was the wife of a consultant psychiatrist with a new Jaguar.

I'd been given a scare and it had done me good.

As I savoured the news once again, I reflected that the tide had finally turned for me in Australia. Good luck was at last starting to flow. I'd got free from the kidnappers. I'd helped to boot Gil Jericho out of professional golf. I'd had the satisfaction of hitting Lee Whitfield on behalf of an old man and his dog. And I'd been instrumental in parting Warren Oxley from his second wife. When I added Lynette's news, I saw that I was riding high. Australia had smiled on me. I was in better financial shape than I'd ever been and I was going home to my family.

It was almost too good to be true. I kept expecting something to spoil it. A tap on the shoulder that made me turn around to face new horrors and anguish.

It was right on cue.

Instead of a tap, it was pounding on my door. It was not Jan Cummings this time. The knock had a menace to it. A formal, demanding, peremptory sound.

A voice came through the door like a battering ram.

'Open up, Mr Saxon!'

'Who is it?'

'Police!'

'What do you want?'

'Open up, sir.'

I resigned myself to the worst and obeyed the order. I could almost feel the handcuffs on my wrists. When I opened the door, I was confronted by two large, glowering policemen who stood side by side. The very sight of their uniforms made me wilt. My run of good fortune was over.

'Mr Saxon?' said one of them.

'Yes.'

'We've been sent as a matter of emergency.'

'It's all right, officer. I'll come quietly.'

'You want to be more careful, sir,' he warned.

'What's the charge?'

'Absent-mindedness.'

'Eh?'

'You left these at the police station.'

He stepped aside to reveal the golf bag he'd been concealing behind him. In the haste of my departure from the police station, I'd completely forgotten them.

The two officers guffawed royally at their little joke. They had made me sweat and that was cause for celebration. I took my bag and joined in the laughter, learning something that my father had never mentioned.

Policemen had a sense of humour as well.

I flew home the next day.

I was needed there.

TOUCH PLAY

Martin Inigo

Mel Edmunds is the world's No. 1 tennis player. He's
also arrogant, conceited, unpopular on the circuit, but
very popular with women. And now he's lying dead in his
hotel bedroom in Monte Carlo, the victim – or so it seems
– of a *crime passionnel*.

Don Hawker, ex-Olympic athlete turned sports journalist,
knows all about the pressures and passions of
international sports. He also knows that Mel's wife Katie
– herself a tennis champion – went on a mysterious
mission the day before her husband was killed. What he
doesn't know is who was *really* sleeping with who, why an
Italian beauty queen is looking so sad, or where the
unpleasant London businessman fits into the picture.

But as the players move to Rome and on to Paris, Hawker
learns a lot more – about another murder, corruption,
blackmail, and serious threats on his own life . . .

0 7474 0103 5
CRIME

THE JUDGE'S SONG

Bernard Bannerman

It was, as Dave Woolf said, 'the sort of thing that doesn't happen in England'. High-court corruption, gangsters, fire-bombs and a bit of murder on the side – all of it against the backdrop of a family drama raging through London, the West Country and the South of France.

It's not the sort of thing that solicitors ought to be investigating. But Woolf is no ordinary solicitor. Back in the legal fold after a spell as a private eye, he's roped into a spot of detection for the usual reasons – an irresistible · fee. Sustained by hefty slugs of Southern Comfort, Camels and his new Aussie sidekick, he's ready to haul a few skeletons out of family cupboards. The trouble is, they're still alive . . .

0 7474 0520 4
CRIME

All Sphere Books are available at your bookshop or newsagent, or can be ordered from the following address:

Sphere Books,
Cash Sales Department,
P.O. Box 11,
Falmouth,
Cornwall TR10 9EN.

Alternatively you may fax your order to the above address. Fax No. 0326 76423.

Payments can be made as follows: Cheque, postal order (payable to Macdonald & Co (Publishers) Ltd) or by credit cards, Visa/Access. Do not send cash or currency. UK customers: please send a cheque or postal order (no currency) and allow 80p for postage and packing for the first book plus 20p for each additional book up to a maximum charge of £2.00.

B.F.P.O. customers please allow 80p for the first book plus 20p for each additional book.

Overseas customers including Ireland, please allow £1.50 for postage and packing for the first book, £1.00 for the second book, and 30p for each additional book.

NAME (Block Letters) ....

ADDRESS ....

....

☐ I enclose my remittance for _____

☐ I wish to pay by Access/Visa Card

Number ☐☐☐☐☐☐☐☐☐☐☐☐☐☐☐☐☐☐☐

Card Expiry Date ☐☐☐☐